A
Way Back
TO YOU

A *Way Back* TO YOU

A Novel by

EMILY GRAY CLAWSON

DESERET
BOOK

Salt Lake City, Utah

Author's photo © 2012 Emily Gray Clawson
Photograph by Tamra Hyde, modernexpressionsphoto.com

© 2013 Emily Gray Clawson

Visit us at DeseretBook.com

Library of Congress Cataloging-in-Publication Data
Clawson, Emily Gray, author.
  A way back to you / Emily Gray Clawson.
    pages cm
  ISBN 978-1-60907-521-7 (paperbound)
1. Widows—Fiction. 2. Domestic fiction. I. Title.
  PS3603.L3845W39 2013
  813'.6—dc23   2013009211

Printed in the United States of America
Edwards Brothers Malloy, Ann Arbor, MI

10   9   8   7   6   5   4   3   2   1

For Richard
You are my everything

Acknowledgments

Many thanks are due to the people who have supported and inspired me in writing this book. I would be greatly remiss if I didn't mention them.

Richard, you have been my strength and my mirror. I love you with all my heart. Ethan, Aria, Isaac, and Abby, it's humbling to know you look to me for direction. You are everything. My parents, siblings, and extended family (Olivia and Mary), thank you for being excited for me and for all your feedback.

Thanks to everyone at Deseret Book for turning a bunch of words on a page into a real, live book. How awesome it is to work with you!

To my friends old and new: Geoff, I'd be a different person if I hadn't met you. Tamra, inside out, you know me, oh, so well. Thanks for loving me anyway. Barbie, you rock. Your strength is inspiring and you keep me young.

To Julie Bellon and Jordan McCollum, love you guys. Thanks for making me look better than I could without you. You teach me something new with every bleeding page. And you're seriously hilarious, too.

For my Knights and Maidens, you all are constantly wowing me with your power, knowledge, and passion. I expect you to change the world. You've already changed mine.

Chapter

1

*I*t had been one of those two-year-old-screaming, dead-battery-at-the-grocery-store, pile-of-bills-in-the-mail days. I fell into bed exhausted with, I'm ashamed to admit, a few chunks of oatmeal still in my hair. The mattress was starting to sag, and I tossed and turned a bit, trying to find a position that didn't put my ribs in contact with the metal springs hidden under just a thin layer of padding. Finally, I managed a semicomfortable position and dozed off. I was awakened abruptly not fifteen minutes later by a wet coughing sound coming from the baby's room. James was throwing up.

Three hours and two sheet changes later, I was ready to try again, this time blissfully free of oatmeal, thanks to the vomit-motivated shower I had taken. I didn't even bother trying for a comfortable position. I could have slept on a bed of hot coals. I just flopped onto the bed, pulled the closest blanket up over me, and rolled over to check the clock. Four a.m. Good. I still had two and a half hours until I had to be up to drive carpool. That was enough time to get through at least one sleep cycle. It could have been worse.

My body didn't agree with that assessment when the alarm went off. It protested strenuously, and I debated keeping the kids home from school just so I could sleep in for another hour. The thought of a nap was the only thing that dissuaded me from that idea. If the kids stayed home, that possibility would be gone. I forced myself out of bed and started our morning routine.

Shelley Inger accosted me in the school parking lot as I was zipping up Mallory's jacket and handing her and Jenna their lunches. She walked toward me with a hip-swinging step that caused her high-heeled boots to click loudly on the asphalt. Her skinny jeans left little to the imagination, and her vividly highlighted hair wisped in the cold wind as she called out my name.

"Anne. There you are, darlin'. I was beginning to wonder if you weren't sleeping in this morning."

Her voice was a little too loud after the night I'd had, but I kissed Jenna and Mallory and sent them off before I turned to smile up at Shelley. She was at least four inches taller than I was, even without the heels. And the hair. So I had to look up quite a ways.

"What are you doin' tonight? You got any big plans?" she asked.

I stifled a groan of exasperation. I had discovered quickly that living in a small town meant that everyone felt entitled to know everyone else's business. I was the one and only widow under sixty in the neighborhood, so I had come to expect the constant stream of judgment, usually masked as sympathy sprinkled liberally by the more officious busybodies who tried to set me up with everything male between the ages of twenty-one and seventy. Shelley was usually the prime perpetrator.

"Oh, yes. Big, *big* plans. I have a mountain of laundry waiting to be done," I quipped, trying to keep things light. My efforts were wasted. Shelley pursed her pink-lined lips in a blend of sympathy and censure.

"Darlin', you really got to get out of that house. I know what you need. Pete has a friend . . ." She stopped and frowned as I groaned out loud. "What? What is the matter with meeting someone? It's been what, three years?"

"Two years and seven months." I didn't like the direction this was going.

"Okay, two and a half years. That's long enough. Eventually you gotta find someone new. Pete's friend is a great guy. He's one of those intellectual types but good looking. *And* he's only been married once— has a little girl close to Jenna's age." She delivered the description as if she were offering me a lottery jackpot.

"Well, that's a relief. That last guy was on, what, his fifth divorce?"

"Sixth, but hey, at least he had money. This one's not rich, but he's probably more your type." She winked. I really couldn't believe I was listening to this. It felt like high school all over again. Not something I was eager to relive. "He's comin' over for dinner tonight, and I know he'd be so excited to meet you. Pete can't stop talking about you."

Now *that* was funny. "Pete, huh? The man who never says more than two words together can't stop talking about me?"

"Okay, it was me. But Pete agreed when I said you were really cute," Shelley said. She looked me over, taking in my sweatshirt and pajama pants, lingering a little longer at my hair. "Maybe you could wear that little black dress?"

My stomach clenched at the thought.

"Shelley, it's really nice for you to invite me, but I don't have a sitter," I said. I'd let this discussion go on long enough. I wanted to get away.

"What about my Megan? She's great with the little ones, and Mallory and Jenna can practically take care of themselves anyway. It's not like you'll be gone overnight . . . unless you really hit it off," she laughed.

I cringed again. She might mean well, but could this conversation go any further downhill?

"Come on, Anne. At least think about it. Dinner's at seven thirty. Okay?" She grinned again and then shimmied off to intercept Mrs. Walsh. Rumor had it that Mr. Walsh had been arrested for driving under the influence, and I guessed Shelley wanted to get the scoop from the source.

I stared after her, resenting her interference even while I envied how easy it was for her to talk to people. I got into my car and turned the key. The engine started on the third try. As I glanced in the rearview mirror to back out, I caught a glimpse of myself. Ugh. My hair was sticking out all over, thanks to sleeping on it wet. No wonder Shelley had been staring at me like that.

"Lovely," I muttered, trying to smooth it. One lock of hair continued to flip out unnaturally like a neon sign flashing the words "She really let herself go." It must have been the sleepless night, or maybe I was getting sick like James, but I had this horrible pain in the pit of my stomach that grew and grew. I thought maybe I was going to throw up, but instead the pain just pushed itself up and out in a huge sob. Tears followed immediately, and I struggled to see as I pulled out of the parking lot.

"Mommy sad?" James asked from his car seat in the back. I stuffed the pain back down and wiped my face, looking around the car for something to blow my nose on. Nothing. I sniffed.

"No, baby," I said in a falsely cheerful tone. "Mommy's fine. I'm just tired. Let's go home and give you a bath, okay?"

James pouted at the suggestion. His little face was so cute that I couldn't help smiling through the tears. I kept up a steady babble of toddler talk for the rest of the drive home. Anything to keep my mind distracted from that black hole looming inside me.

Two hours later I had James fed, bathed, and down for a nap. As I started another load of laundry, I came across one of Mitch's old T-shirts. Mallory had been using it to sleep in, and I'd seen it dozens of times in the laundry. I moved to toss it into the washer, but my hands wouldn't let go. The water kept filling the drum, detergent already foaming, but I couldn't make my fingers release that shirt.

There was a stain near the hem, just a smudge of darker gray. I didn't know what had caused it, but a flash of a memory surfaced—Mitch opening my car door at the grocery store while he tugged his jacket on and I caught just a glimpse of that small stain on the hem of his shirt. It was an insignificant memory, but it sucked all of the air from my chest.

All of the anguish, the loss, the emptiness washed over me. For more than two and a half years I'd done everything possible to avoid facing this reality. Maybe it would hurt less as time went on, or maybe I'd find that it had crept in gradually, softened by time. I don't know exactly what I'd thought, or if I'd even thought at all. I'd just reacted to protect myself. Now it was clear just how false any of those ideas were. The pain hadn't lessened. It had intensified as if it were breeding in the hidden recesses of my mind. Now that it was loose, it attacked mercilessly, crushing me to the floor of my laundry room with its weight.

I couldn't catch my breath. My heart and lungs begged for oxygen, but there wasn't room for any air to enter. Every nook and cranny of my body was suddenly filled with the fact that Mitch was really and truly gone.

Finally I sucked in a lungful of air, trying to clear the drumming pain away. But when I blew it out, it was nothing more than a small, piteous cry. I clutched the shirt to my chest and curled up beside the laundry baskets and let the grief have its way with me.

I'd spent the last two and a half years trying to keep the pain of losing Mitch at bay. It seemed like there was never a good time to really face it. I had the girls to care for. Mallory had been nine and Jenna five when Mitch died, and it seemed like all my energy went into filling their needs and helping them through the horrifying experience of losing their father. Then, just weeks after his death, I discovered I was pregnant. Everything changed at that point as I began focusing my efforts and energy into making sure that Mitch's new baby would be healthy and loved.

Now, I'd been fighting this moment for so long that I thought I'd dealt with his death. I really did. How wrong I'd been. Now that the dam had burst, I didn't know if I would ever be able to stop crying. Oh, how grateful I was that the children couldn't see me like this.

They needed me to be strong for them, but there was no strength inside me right now. For some crazy reason, Shelley Inger popped into my head with her comment about my little black dress, and that started off a fresh wave of sobs. She couldn't have realized that I had bought that dress for Mitch's funeral. The thought of wearing it to impress a man was nauseating.

Minutes passed, then an hour, and I still couldn't regain control. I gave up on trying to accomplish anything and just staggered back to my bedroom, collapsing on my bed. When James woke up, I put him in front of a movie and gave him sugary cereal to snack on. He stared at my red, blotchy face and wrapped his little arms around me, trying to comfort me in his baby way. That broke through the little bubble

I'd managed to survive in since he woke up, and I started crying again. Luckily he was distracted by the brightly colored cereal and the animated figures on the screen, and I lay on the couch and cried, covering my face with a pillow when I couldn't keep it quiet. By two thirty I knew I would have to pick up the girls soon. How could I drive like this? *How can I live like this?* my heart keened.

I was utterly defeated. I called Shelley and asked if she could give the girls a ride home. I knew I was risking a mountain of gossip, but I didn't care anymore.

"Sure, darlin', but you sound awful. Are you okay?" she asked, her voice dripping with concern and curiosity.

"I think I'm getting sick," I lied. What was I supposed to tell her, anyway?

"Oh, okay. Well, I'll drop them off." There was a pause, and I could tell there was something more she wanted to say. "This is just an excuse to get out of dinner tonight, isn't it?" I fought back a fresh batch of wails and managed to answer.

"It really isn't. I'm just not well today." That last part was definitely the truth.

"Okay. I'll see you in an hour," she said. I thanked her and told her good-bye. It wasn't until I hung up the phone that I realized from her comment that she was actually planning on coming in. I stumbled to the bathroom mirror and surveyed the damage. My hair was still sticking out all over, and my face was puffy. I was thirty-eight, but I looked at least ten years older. It shocked me into silence, my tears halted by the realization that it wasn't just about the crying today. I'd been letting myself slowly decay since Mitch had died. I sank to the floor of the bathroom.

Chapter

2

*S*helley found me there an hour later. I hadn't moved the entire time. I heard James get hold of the box of cereal and go crazy, scattering bits of cereal all over the living room. I didn't bother to stop him. I didn't check on him. I didn't even cry. I sat.

"Darlin'? Anne? Honey, are you okay?"

I couldn't muster any energy to answer her. All I kept thinking over and over again was, *Mitch is gone, and I'm old.* The thought ran like ticker tape across my mind, taking up any space there might have been to form another coherent thought. Somewhere in my mind I knew that it was ridiculous. Who cared how old I looked? I didn't need to look young and beautiful to do laundry and make lunches and drive to school. That was my life. Why did I need to be young, anyway? Still, the thought never left, and I couldn't seem to answer Shelley. She stared at me for a long moment.

"Mallory," Shelley called after a long moment, "pack up some things. You kids are coming to stay with me. Your mom needs a break."

I heard Mallory and Jenna cheer. For some unfathomable reason they loved Shelley's house.

"You are taking the weekend off, Anne. The kids can stay with me. You need to get out of this house, you hear me?"

Get out of the house? Where on earth would I go? *Mitch is gone, and I'm old. How can I leave? I'm so old.* I didn't answer. I couldn't even seem to care that she was taking my children for an entire weekend. I just sat and stared at the bathroom cabinet. I'd never noticed the scuff marks on the corner. I didn't answer.

"That's it," Shelley said. "I'm calling your mother."

That stirred something inside of me.

"No. Don't call her. I'm okay," I said, but I knew my voice sounded completely lifeless. *Mitch is dead, and I'm old.* "Mitch is dead, and I'm old," I said out loud. Then the tears came back, and they were more overwhelming than ever.

"I know, darlin'," Shelley said, softly wrapping me in a warm hug. She smelled really good. I couldn't remember the last time I wore perfume. I cried harder.

Shelley left me there on the floor while she gathered up the bags Mallory had packed. Then I heard her on the phone, but I couldn't muster any energy to care if she really were calling my mother. She came back a couple of minutes later.

"Okay, Anne. Pull yourself together long enough to kiss your kiddos." Her voice was firm, and I obeyed.

I nodded and sniffed, scrubbed my face with my sweatshirt, and tried to plaster a semblance of a smile on my face. Shelley ushered the kids into the bathroom. James and Jenna were excited, but the worry on Mallory's face made her look five years older. She was so much like me, and in that moment I knew just what I had been doing to her.

"Hey, babies. You guys are going to go have a slumber party at Shelley's house, okay? Mom's got some stuff to take care of. I'll see you on . . ." I glanced at Shelley, who mouthed *Sunday*. "I'll see you on Sunday. Have a ton of fun, okay?" I kissed James and Jenna and hugged Mallory.

"I'll be fine, honey. Please have fun, okay?" I whispered in her ear. I smoothed her dark blonde hair, exactly the same color as mine, and cupped her cheek in my hand. She hesitated at first, but I managed a weak smile, and she nodded.

"Okay, kids, go get in the car," Shelley said, shooing them from the bathroom. "I'll be right there. I just have to tell your mom one more thing."

The ticker tape in my mind changed. *Mitch is dead, I'm old, and*

I'm making my kids old, too. The tears started again, quieter this time but no less desperate.

"All right, darlin', this is the deal. Your mom is going to be here in an hour, so pack a few things. You are going to stay with her for the weekend. You are going to get yourself together and come back and stop living like a dead woman, okay?"

Shelley's pink lipstick didn't look quite so garish, and I was filled with sudden affection for her. I had lumped her in with the other nosy busybodies of this town. They were only attracted to me because of the tragedy I'd been through. I guess they thought it somehow made them important to report to their friends all the goings-on of my life. Now I saw that she was genuinely concerned about me. It meant a lot.

"Thanks, Shelley," I managed to get out through the tears.

She nodded and patted my face.

"Sure, darlin'. Don't worry about the kids. They'll be fine."

"Okay."

She smiled and left. I heard the door shut and the car pull out of the driveway, and I silently promised my children that somehow things would change. I didn't ever want to see that look in Mallory's eyes again.

When Mom pulled up, I was waiting on the front porch, a packed bag at my feet. The Cadillac door opened, and I braced myself, promising that I wouldn't lose my temper. Mom emerged, perfect as always in sleek gray slacks and a coral sweater set that had probably cost almost as much as my mortgage for the month. She looked as if she had just come from a gallery opening or some benefit luncheon, but I knew there didn't need to be an occasion. She dressed like that to buy groceries. She perched her sunglasses on top of her head and walked toward the porch. I grabbed my bag and stood up, meeting her before she could reach the stairs. Her knees weren't what they used to be. *Mitch is dead, I'm old, and I'm making my children old.*

I didn't wait for her to speak. I had no energy for an argument, nor did I have a desire to listen to gushing sympathy or stinging judgment, the only two methods of communication we had. I just greeted her with a kiss on the cheek and went to the car. I opened the back door to put my bag in, but the trunk popped open with a touch of her remote.

"Oh, did you want me to put my bag in the trunk?" I asked.

"Oh, honey. You can put it wherever you like. If you want it in the backseat, that's okay, I guess," she said sweetly.

"No, really. If it bothers you for me to put it on the seat, I can put it in the trunk."

"Don't be silly. Why would that bother me?"

"Okay. I'll put it in the backseat, then." I moved to swing the bag onto the seat, but her voice stopped me.

"It's just that your father recently had the leather conditioned. It keeps it supple, you know. But I'm sure that a bag wouldn't cause any damage. There aren't any metal pieces on the outside, are there?" She trailed off as I closed the back door and put the bag in the trunk, slamming it shut. It was always like this.

I got in the passenger side and braced myself for the drive. It was only twenty minutes away, too close for me to have an excuse for not visiting more often. It might not have been very far, but Mom's driving had been the source of many jokes for my siblings and me throughout the years. Mom thought she was an excellent driver, which meant that she prided herself on being able to see through the evil designs and cunning plans of those around her, making a preemptive strike when necessary.

We weaved in and out of traffic between my house and the freeway, and Mom started to tell me all about the people in the old neighborhood, reporting on illnesses and deaths and family scandals. With her friends she was careful never to appear gossipy, but with me, Hannah, Dan, and Rachel, my brother and sisters, she felt it her duty to keep us apprised of everything that happened to the people we had known as children. I let her words wash over me, taking in some of it but mostly just listening to the voice in my head. *Mitch is dead, you're old, and you are making your kids old, too.* What was I even doing here in this car with my mother? How was spending the weekend with her going to help me? I started feeling sick to my stomach, and I wondered if I was catching whatever James had. That snapped my head up. I hadn't told Shelley that James was sick.

"What's the matter, dear?" Mom asked, taking in my worried face and my taut posture.

"James was throwing up last night. I can't leave the kids with Shelley. I don't know what I was thinking. I need to get home." I started fishing through my pockets for my cell phone.

"Mallory told Shelley, Anne. She's prepared for it, and you are coming home with me," Mom said. "You need this time away. You can sleep in your old room, and I'll make you pancakes in the morning."

I slumped back in my seat. Mom's pancakes were delicious, but her cooking was also part of the reason I had lived my teenage years as a fat kid. I was strict about avoiding carbohydrates now. As for my old room, when Hannah went away to college it was turned into an "exercise room," meaning there was a treadmill in the corner. A sofa bed had replaced the bed, and my siblings and I jokingly named it "The Rack" because it was so bad on the back. On the rare occasions that Mallory and Jenna had slept over, back before Mitch's death, they had always preferred sleeping on the floor in the game room to enduring The Rack. This was going to be just a lovely weekend. Maybe I really would get sick. At least that way I would have an excuse to stay shut in that room without intrusion.

By the time we pulled into the garage of my parents' house, I wondered if I had any more gray hairs from enduring the car trip. Why had I agreed to let her pick me up? *Oh, yeah,* I thought, *because I'm virtually catatonic.* Could someone really be classified as catatonic if she is aware of behaving that way? *Mitch is dead, I'm old, and I'm making my children old, too.*

Dad was in the living room, sitting on the couch with his laptop, working quietly while he watched a Clint Eastwood movie, something with guns and cars. He glanced back and forth from the computer to the TV screen frequently, managing to spend equal time with both and typing faster one-handed than most able-bodied secretaries. When he noticed me, he smiled and moved his laptop to the sofa, paused his movie with the remote, and got up to greet me.

"Hi, baby cakes," he said, wrapping me in a lopsided bear hug and almost squishing the air out of my lungs. "Glad you could be here. Why don't we put your things away, and then you can come and watch a movie on the big screen with me?"

"Thanks, Dad, but I'm really tired. I think I'm just going to take a nap. I didn't get much sleep last night," I said.

"Hank, don't bother her. She's here to get some rest," Mom said sternly. "We won't bother you at all, honey. You just go ahead and do whatever you need to. I put some sheets and blankets in your room, and there are clean towels in the bathroom." Dad shrugged and then winked at me.

"Let me take your bag, Annie," he said, reaching out for it. I gripped it tighter.

"That's sweet, Dad, but you go ahead and watch the movie. It looks really good," I said. There was no way I was letting him try to carry the bag upstairs. Dad had lost an arm in Vietnam. He'd always been a strong man, more capable than most men with two arms, but in the last couple of years his balance had become so bad he'd fallen several times, once breaking his leg. The thought of him walking up the stairs without being able to hold on to a railing was too scary. Still, he was also proud and hated it when someone said he couldn't do something. I tried to always make it seem to be just my preference. It was a skill I wished Mom would pick up on.

"Hank, don't you dare try carrying that bag upstairs. You'll fall and break a hip. Then where will I be?" she groused.

Dad rolled his eyes, winked at me again, and turned back to his movie but not before I saw a flicker of hurt in his eyes.

"Have a good nap, baby cakes," he said over his shoulder as I headed up the stairs.

"Thanks, Dad."

My old room was at the end of the hall, thankfully as far from my parents' room as possible. I had asked for it for that exact reason when we'd moved into this house twenty-five years ago. As I opened the door, nostalgia flooded over me. Little had changed besides the furniture. The walls were pale pink, and the carpet was a dated dark blue, although I'd rarely seen the carpet when I lived here. It had always been buried under a mountain of clothes, books, and papers. The same pink-and-blue floral curtains hung in the window, faded less than I would have expected. Usually when I was in this room, it was on a quick errand to get something out of the closet, which now held the overflow of my mom's closet, or to gather up the children after a visit, and it seemed like I hadn't really looked at it in a long time.

I put my bag down against the wall and sat down on The Rack. It wasn't too bad as a sofa. Maybe I'd just sleep on it like that, without making it out into a bed. Mom had placed a neat stack of Ralph Lauren sheets and pillowcases and one of my grandmother's handmade quilts on the end of the sofa. I fingered the luxurious linens.

"Who does she think she's fooling?" I asked myself. My mom hadn't always been obsessed with shopping and brand names and fashion. She'd been a stay-at-home mom, like me, broke but happy. Or at least that's what I'd always thought. But when Dad's investment portfolio had started paying off, she had been like a starving woman suddenly unleashed on an all-you-can-eat buffet, and she hadn't stopped since. It occurred to me that maybe she felt just as empty as I did. It was while I stared at the sheets, the indication that my mother was searching for something to fill her, that I realized we were the same. It wasn't just Mitch I'd lost. I'd lost myself, too. I was mourning us both.

The tears started again, but they were quiet this time, and when they faded, they left me relaxed. I curled up under my grandmother's quilt and fell asleep just as the sun was setting.

Chapter

3

I was surprised at how well I slept. The Rack was more comfortable than I could have imagined, and with the lack of sleep the night before added to the fact that I had no kids to wake me up, I slept through the night for the first time in years. The sun was just peeking through the curtains when I rolled onto my back and stretched luxuriously. I felt surprisingly refreshed and awake. The old clock on the wall said it was six thirty. I guessed my body couldn't make it past my usual waking time. I thought about trying to go back to sleep. I was really comfortable, but the smell of pancakes was already wafting up the stairs. My stomach growled ferociously.

A door slammed in the hall, and I heard small feet running lightly down the stairs. Who could that have been? I wondered if my parents had picked up the kids the night before. That thought had me instantly up. I felt so much better today. I must have just really been tired yesterday. I wanted my children to see that I was fine and to know that things really were going to get better. I started toward the door but tripped and almost fell as I stumbled across a huge pile of clothes on the floor. I caught myself and stared around in complete surprise. In place of The Rack was a twin-sized brass daybed with porcelain finials, and all around me, covering every surface of the floor, dresser, nightstand, and windowsill, was an unholy mess.

"What in the world?" I muttered.

I picked my way through the disaster area, shoving crumpled papers, books, shoes, and candy wrappers out of the way until I could see the dark blue carpet underneath, and then I caught sight of my toenails. They were painted in a glaring rainbow of neon hues, five different colors, one for each toe.

"Mom?" I called out.

"Mom!" I heard Mallory yell from downstairs. "He's taking the last pancake! It's not fair." I stumbled and tripped my way to the door and wrenched it open. Who had taken her pancakes? James? He wasn't big enough to eat that much. Surely it wasn't my dad. I'd figure out the mess later. And the toes. I was eager to see my kids.

"Mom!" Mallory wailed again.

"I'm coming. Hold on a second, honey," I called. I was out of breath from hurrying down the hall and the stairs. I could hear a fight starting in the kitchen.

"Give that back!"

"You already had three. I'm still hungry!" There was a grunt and the squeal of a chair skidding across the floor and sounds like a wrestling match was starting.

"Kids, stop fighting, I'll be right . . ." I stopped as I turned the corner. It wasn't Mallory and James or even Jenna. A boy and girl looked up at me as I skidded to a halt in front of the table.

"Who asked you, Annie?" the boy asked, sticking his tongue out as far as it could reach. Then he resumed his tussle with the girl, both of them trying to grab the last pancake off the table. Mom came through from the dining room, and my jaw dropped open at her appearance.

"Daniel Henry May, you give that pancake to your sister. You've already had yours."

She swatted his hands away and put the pancake on the girl's plate. Rachel. My eyes broke away from my brother and sister. As children. I knew my jaw was gaping open, but I couldn't close it. Mom was bustling around, clearing dirty dishes and rinsing them off in the sink. Her hair was dark brown and past her shoulders, pulled into a messy ponytail, and she was dressed in a pair of jeans and a yellow T-shirt, from the bargain store by the looks of them. She wasn't wearing any makeup or jewelry. Her face was so young. Her cheeks had a natural blush, and her skin was soft and smooth. She didn't look at me as she brushed past me to gather more dirty plates.

"Mom! You are so beautiful!" I stammered, awed by the transformation.

She didn't turn. Dan strode away from the table, grumbling under his breath. I thought I caught the phrase "crazy women," but I wasn't sure.

"There aren't any more pancakes," Mom said without turning, a biting edge to her voice. "I'm sorry, but if you don't get up earlier, you'll never have time for breakfast before school." Her voice sounded weary, defeated.

"School? It's Saturday. The girls don't have school today. Mom, really, you look amazing!"

I couldn't get over how gorgeous she was. She slammed down the dishcloth, soapy water slapping out of the sink and over the counter.

"Annabelle May, don't you start with me today. I don't have it in me. Not after last night. I just can't . . ." She dropped her arms wearily to her sides. "I don't want to fight. Please. We'll figure it all out, but at least just get ready for school, okay?" she pleaded. My mouth worked silently. *What?*

Mom stared at me for a minute longer and then dried her hands on a dishtowel and swept past me.

"If you and Hannah want a ride, you need to be ready in twenty minutes. Otherwise, you'll have to walk," Mom said as she passed, still not looking at me. "Dan, Rachel, Hannah, are you guys ready? The bus will be here in twenty minutes," she called as she ran up the stairs.

I was dumbstruck. I turned to follow. As I passed the living room I noticed The Rack in its place of honor under the window. It was no longer faded and worn but vibrant and new-looking. A panicky feeling began in the pit of my stomach. I ran back upstairs after Mom, gasping by the time I reached the top. The feeling intensified.

"Mom, where are you?" I called.

"In here," she answered. I entered her room, and the first edges of hysteria began to creep over me when I saw the peach tricot quilt draped over her bed. No Ralph Lauren sheets here. This was starting to look intensely familiar. Mom was standing in front of her mirror, brushing her hair into a more orderly ponytail. I walked nervously up behind her, my heart pounding out of my chest. When I caught sight of my reflection, I screamed, and the floor tilted up to meet me as I collapsed in shock, the image of myself as a sixteen-year-old swimming in front of my eyes.

My first thought when I woke up was that it was all a dream. Then I realized that I'd just passed out and yet I was still here. Was it even possible to pass out in a dream? Now that I was paying closer attention, I could feel the extra pounds layered around my torso, my arms, my legs. I wondered how I'd missed it before. No wonder I'd been so out of breath. Possible or not, here I was.

"She's obviously not feeling well. Let's just let her stay home, and she'll be fine tomorrow," Dad said from somewhere far overhead.

"She's just trying to get out of that algebra test. I told you she would do this, Hank. It's always something."

Mom was on the verge of tears. I could hear it in the way her voice was softer than normal. She always did that when she was trying not to cry.

"Maybe, maybe. But Dr. Santos will be able to help, I'm sure of it. Let's just get through this day, and things will look better. 'Today is the first day of the rest of your life.' Remember?"

I groaned at the sappy saying, still not really registering the rest, and then instantly regretted it when they both started talking to me at once.

"Get up and get dressed for school right now, Annie," Mom said.

"Go back to bed, baby cakes," Dad said at the same time.

"Hank," Mom warned, "you have to stop babying her. She's sixteen. It's time she started acting like it. If you would just expect a little more from her, maybe we wouldn't be dealing with all of this . . ."

"I'm getting up," I said loudly before she could light into Dad anymore.

He reached down and pulled me up easily, even with the extra weight. I stared at him, and my eyes went wide. He was so strong. "Dad, you are amazing, you know that?"

Mom sighed and rolled her eyes at me. "Here she goes again," she said, but I didn't stay to listen. I hurried to my room to brush my hair, so thick and long, back into a ponytail. This was a dream, I was sure, but going along with it seemed easier than listening to my mother chastising my father until I woke up. I'd had high school dreams before, and they usually ended in my not remembering my locker combination and then wandering into my classes in my underwear. This was just a more twisted Freudian manifestation than normal, probably brought on by my bout of emotional hysteria yesterday. The sooner I got this over with, the better.

I couldn't remember exactly how I used to do my hair on mornings when I was late. The usual ritual of mousse, blow dryer, curling iron, teasing, and voluminous amounts of hairspray that I remembered was definitely out of the question today, as were the layers of carefully applied mascara, so I hoped the ponytail was okay. Still, I thought I looked pretty amazing as I surveyed myself. My face was rounder, not just from the extra thirty pounds but also just because I was so young! My skin was much softer and had a healthy glow, even though it was marked by a couple of blemishes. I dabbed a touch of concealer in a few strategic places, feeling pleased that I was wearing makeup at all. I hadn't worn any since Mitch had died, except for Sundays at church, and even then it was usually mascara and lip gloss and not much else.

The clothes were hilarious, but I managed to find some jeans in the pile on the floor that weren't quite as slashed and bleached and tight in the ankle as the others and a green sweater that seemed vaguely familiar. The pants were too tight, though, and too short, barely coming to my ankle. I figured that was why they weren't as worn out as the others. They didn't fit anymore. After trying on a couple of other pairs,

I was reminded that I had worn them that way on purpose for some crazy reason. I had to lie down on the bed to zip them up. At least the sweater was baggy and hid the bulge around my middle created by my pants. Finally I found a pair of sneakers crammed halfway under the bed, and, lo and behold, there was a pair of clean socks actually folded together in the otherwise empty top drawer of my dresser.

Mom was waiting impatiently at the bottom of the stairs with her purse slung over her shoulder, and she looked vaguely surprised when I walked downstairs. She probably had thought I wouldn't show.

"Let's go," I said with a smile and walked past her to the garage door.

She made a huffing noise as I passed but then followed behind me. I hit the door opener on the wall out of long ingrained habit, and as the light came on I gasped and started laughing.

"I totally forgot about the Wagon! This is classic!" I ran around and opened the passenger door to the blue station wagon and climbed inside, buckling my seat belt. My mom looked at me strangely as she got in and started the car. The radio came on, and I started to laugh again as the B-52s came blaring out of the speakers. I felt so alive and young and full of energy, and the song reflected my mood. I turned up the radio and sang along.

"Roam if you want to! Roam around the world!" Mom quickly snapped the radio off. We drove in silence for a few minutes until Mom glanced over and saw my bewildered expression.

"You know I hate loud music in the car, Annie," she explained with a sigh.

I was surprised to hear the sorrow in her voice. We were all so young and healthy. What was there to be sad about?

"Mom, what is the matter? So far all I've done today is tell you how nice you look and sing along with the radio, and you've been completely annoyed with me. What's the big problem?" I was surprised at how upset I sounded. My emotions were much closer to the surface than I had realized, but I was still surprised when she actually burst into tears, crying like I had been crying yesterday.

"How . . . can . . . you . . . ask me . . . that?" she managed to squeak out between sobs. "You think that you can pull a stunt like that, and we are supposed to just forget it and be happy today? I don't know if you were serious or if it was just a cry for attention, but you've got us all in upheaval, and then you act like it's just nothing. Seriously, Annie? What am I supposed to be like today? Am I supposed to be happy and joyful because you threatened to kill yourself? What do you want me to think? I'm sure whatever I've been doing is completely wrong, so, by all means, please tell me how I'm supposed to be handling a doozie like that."

She was yelling now and waving her hand, nearly losing control of the car as we came to a stop in front of the school. A couple of kids darted away from the curb just in time.

Suddenly the earlier mention of Dr. Santos and the algebra test all came together, and I knew what today was. My stomach twisted into a painful knot. Why did I have to dream about today? Why couldn't it have been the day I got my first bike for Christmas or the day that Dad and Grandpa took me fishing at Spirit Lake and I caught a huge rainbow trout? No, today was the day after the day that I had written a ridiculously melodramatic note to Sam Harris, a guy I had a huge crush on, telling him that I was going to kill myself by taking an overdose of prescription medication belonging to my dad. Today was the day after I had been picked up by my hysterical mother, who had been called by Sam and told of my plans. Today was the day after I had met with our family's bishop for two hours while he counseled and prayed with me, hoping to help me find the way back to my faith. Today was the worst day of my years as a teenager.

It's funny. You'd think that threatening to commit suicide would make more of an impression on you through your life, but as I became an adult and grew out of the crazy, overwrought emotionalism of youth and started to care more about other people than I did about myself, I had buried that memory as a mere embarrassment that I was grateful we had all survived. My parents loved me anyway, and my younger sisters and brother proved to be even wilder than I was, so I had become the golden child by the time I was married at twenty years old. I had never told Mitch of the incident, knowing that it was nothing more than the worst, most selfish plea for attention that anyone could ever perpetrate on the people they love. I didn't want him to think of me as that kind of person. In the end it was just swept under the rug, and it disappeared from my life and from my mind. Or so I had thought.

Now I was coming face to face with the pain of it all in a way I had never understood before. As we sat in front of the high school, the kids pouring inside in answer to the first bell that had just rung, I watched my mom, broken and sobbing at the steering wheel. I was flooded with a remorse so strong that I wondered that it didn't cripple me. Instead of cringing away from it, though, I reached out and put my arms around my mom and hugged her to me. She resisted at first, but then she went limp and she clung to me, too.

"Mom, I'm so sorry. I was an idiot. I wasn't really going to do it, and it was so selfish and stupid of me to put you through that. I love you, and I promise that I'm not in danger. I'm pulling it together, okay?"

She continued to cry, but it sounded softer now. "Why, Annie? Why would you even pretend something like that? What were you thinking?"

"It's the worst reason possible. I was just crazy in love with Sam, and I was a drama queen. I had no idea that I would find someone like Mitch and lose all the weight and feel good about myself. I had no idea how happy I could be with someone else. I was just always obsessed with Sam." I stopped as she opened her mouth in surprise.

"Who is Mitch?" she asked, trying to keep up.

"Never mind. I just mean that I was so caught up with Sam that I didn't think I could ever find anyone else I would love more. It's ridiculous. I mean, it's not like that kind of behavior would ever get a person what they wanted. I seriously don't know what possessed me. I promise, though, I'm not going to harm myself or anyone else. I'm going to grow up and find a great man and get married and have three kids, and we are going to live in the Valley and visit you every Sunday, and I'm going to teach Primary and be PTA president." I didn't add that I would lose my husband to a brain aneurysm and stop being in the PTA or teaching Primary. Or showering. That wasn't what she needed to hear right now.

"PTA, huh?" Mom said, with just a hint of a smile. Then the sternness returned. "Well, we'll see. You better get to class. You're already late, and you need to ace that algebra test if you are going to pass the class. Do you need a ride home?" Mom might have been back to business, but she seemed lighter somehow, and I hoped that she could know that I really meant it when I said I was sorry. It was one of my biggest regrets in life that I hadn't ever told her just how sorry I was. I had just tried to forget it.

"I think I'll walk. I need the exercise," I said, ignoring the stunned look that crossed her face at that statement. I climbed out of the car and walked toward the school.

Chapter
4

I understand that it's nearly midterm, Mrs. Dennis, but I really need a copy of my school schedule this morning. I know it's a pain, but I promised my father I'd pick it up," I pleaded.

Mrs. Dennis regarded me with a suspicious eye, finally stalking off to the filing cabinet at the back of the room. Filing cabinets? I had forgotten how much harder things were without the Internet. There wasn't even a computer on Mrs. Dennis's desk. Weird. She shuffled through a few drawers and then returned with a half sheet of paper.

"You'll need to write down the information. This is my only copy," she said.

"Thanks. I really appreciate it," I said. I dug in the gigantic tote bag that I had grabbed on the way out the door, trying to find a pencil, and finally emerged with a spiral notebook and blue pen. As I copied down the schedule, I had to laugh. The ink was a violent shade of green. I had forgotten about my propensity for brightly colored pens. Mrs. Dennis eyed me sharply at the sound, and I hurried to finish and get out of her hair.

We had a block schedule, even-numbered classes on one day and odds on the other, but Mom had pointed out that I had an algebra test today. According to my schedule, that meant today was an odd day. Luckily, Algebra was seventh period. I had time to study. I hiked my bag onto my shoulder and headed out into the hall. I had spent too long in the office, but it was still first period, and the halls were empty. As I walked upstairs toward my first class, World History, I marveled at the fact that I was actually here again. Yes, I'd had those high school dreams before, but nothing as vivid and long-lasting as this. Everything was brown—the carpet, the walls, the wooden railings, the light tan lockers. Everything except the doors, which were painted bright yellow and green, the school colors. With every step I took I felt my heart sink lower and lower in my chest. I had walked in here thinking I could breeze through the day, making my mother happy. Now that I was actually here, all the memories of high school started to roll over me. The real ones. The ones that involved feeling like an insignificant nobody unless that was replaced by feeling like a hideous pariah.

I looked down again at my jeans and T-shirt and thought about my hair and makeup. This morning, when I was getting ready, I had dismissed all of that as inconsequential, a waste of time. Suddenly I remembered why I went through that ritual every day. It was my armor, and I had come to school without it. Dream or not, I had a feeling this wasn't going to be pretty.

I made it to the third floor just as the bell rang. Doors burst outward, and a stream of humanity, in all of its strange varieties, boiled into the hall. My jaw dropped as I stared at the outlandish figures that I had all but forgotten. My small-town school was relatively sedate compared to those in more metropolitan areas, with most kids dressed simply and conservatively, but there were still plenty of extreme examples to turn my head. Kids with spiked mohawks and studded leather collars, kids in cowboy hats and huge belt buckles, and kids with ultralong, straight hair and ripped Kiss T-shirts. Even the "normal" kids stood out, the boys with their high-top sneakers and the girls with their big hair. Mall hair, we had called it back then . . . uh, back now, I guessed. I backed up against the wall, trying to avoid being trampled. I was totally unprepared for this.

"Annie! There you are. You missed World Hiss. It was completely lame. Mr. Croft talked for like twenty minutes about some German spy or something. I had no idea what he was actually talking about. Where were you? I tried to call last night, and your mom said you weren't feeling well. Are you sick? Is it the flu?"

That was a voice that I could never forget. Corrie. I turned to see her bouncing toward me, her voice audible over the crowd, even though her head usually wasn't. She wasn't quite five feet tall, but she had more energy and words inside of her than any two other girls combined. My eyes filled with tears at the aching familiarity of the scene, of having my best friend that close to me. We had lost touch only two years out of high school, when I met Mitch and she moved across the country to try to become an actress. I'd heard through the grapevine, meaning my mother talking to her father, that she was involved in drugs and an abusive relationship that I knew, though her father didn't, had started in high school. Eventually she had been so strung out she couldn't keep an apartment. Her father was still trying to discover what had happened to her. Now here she was chattering away in front of me, her permed hair almost vibrating with her energy.

" . . . and then I told her that you were probably just getting a cold or something but she insisted that you were going to be hospitalized. Apparently your sister said something to Angela about there being an emergency last night and I told her 'no way' because you totally would have called me if it was anything serious and now that you're here you can show her that you are totally fine and I can rub it in her face. She's such a cow . . ."

"Wait, Corrie. Who told you that?" I managed to interrupt.

"I told you: Jenny Smoot. She thinks she knows everything, just because her dad works for the school district, but I peeked at her English essay last week when she passed it up front, and she definitely had some major spelling errors and I think that she just . . ."

"Corrie, hold on," I said, trying to head off another massive run-on sentence. "She said that Hannah told her there was an emergency last night?"

"Yeah. So was there?" she asked with surprising brevity.

I didn't want to lie to Corrie, but I also remembered just how loose that fast tongue was. I tried to remember if I'd told her about my "suicide attempt" then, twenty years ago, but the details were fuzzy.

I decided to err on the side of safety. I was also going to have to deal with Hannah and her big mouth. We were only ten months apart, but the closeness in age had never done much to help our relationship. If anything, it made things more strained between us. She seemed to be always watching and waiting for me to do something wrong so she could run to Mom and Dad and get some mileage out of it.

I shoved my sister issues to the back of my mind and focused on Corrie. What had she asked me? Oh, yeah. Something about my past, no, my current emotional state.

"I'm totally fine," I said. *Well, not really. I'm experiencing an overly long dream or maybe a hallucination, and I'm starting to freak out just a tiny bit.* I left all of that out. "I'm here, and I have to study for that algebra test before seventh period, and if we don't hurry, we are going to be late for . . ." What was next on my schedule? I started digging in my bag for the paper I had written my schedule on. Corrie was eyeing me.

"For Music Theory? Seriously, Annie, are you okay?" she asked. "If you are sick, I can take you to the nurse and have her call your mom. I know you guys are like fighting or something, but I'm sure she'd want you to go home if you're sick. She can't be that much of a . . ."

"I'm fine. Really. Let's go to class, okay?"

She shrugged and bounced toward the stairs that I had just come up. Three flights up and now three flights down. I was out of breath from trying to keep up with Corrie and her dizzying energy as she bounded down half the stairs and then ran back up two or three to tell me something, mostly about Jesse, her current boyfriend. How on earth had I managed to go up and down these stairs so many times every day and not lose weight? Or hang out with Corrie, for that matter. I felt like I was burning calories just being near her.

We really were going to be late to class, though, so I hurried as much as I could, cursing my too-tight jeans that made it so much harder for me to take a good deep breath. I was grateful for Corrie's guidance toward the end of the school, but as we proceeded toward the music rooms, I felt my heart speed up. I knew exactly where we were going. This had been my favorite place in high school, and I felt a sense of homecoming that was surprising. For the first time in two and a half years, I experienced a feeling of anticipation, of something good right around the corner. Literally.

We walked around the corner, and there was the door to the band room, the location for our music theory lessons, the place where I had played piano for a couple of different classes. The place where I had first met Sam.

"Sam!" I blurted out, skidding to a halt. I could not go in there. Not today!

Corrie paused in the act of opening the door. She looked at my face with sympathy.

"Annie, we don't have to do this every time, do we? Just act naturally. He's just a guy, just like any other guy. Come on, we're late." She grabbed my hand and tugged me forward. She didn't seem to get that I really couldn't face him after what I had done that day . . . yesterday. She continued to tug on my arm, not making much progress considering the difference in our sizes, but making a valiant effort.

A couple of last-minute arrivals scooted through the door, weaving around us. They looked vaguely familiar as they viewed the scene that we were making. One of them must have mentioned it in class because Mr. Allan came to the door.

"Is there a problem, Miss May? Miss Crump?" Corrie dropped my hand and spun to face him.

"No, Mr. Allan. Annie and I were just coming in. Right, Annie?" I nodded mutely, feeling numb, and allowed myself to be ushered inside.

And there he was. Sam.

Chapter

5

I was shocked, actually shocked, like a bolt of electricity running through my body from my toes and fingers inward to my stomach and then out through my head, as I looked at Sam sitting in the front of the room, three steps down the terraced rows from where I stood. The door was in the back of the room, so all I could see were his shoulders and hair and a bit of his profile, but it was enough to knock the wind out of me.

Corrie rolled her eyes at me and tugged me toward my seat in the back. I stumbled after her, trying to keep my lungs working and my heart beating and simultaneously dreading and longing for him to turn around and look at me. This was ridiculous!

I sank into my seat, and Mr. Allan moved back to the front of the room and started diagramming intervals on the blackboard. The class of twenty-three students all began copying quietly onto their manuscript paper, and I opened my bag to dig out my supplies and follow suit. It took me twice as long as it should have to copy the intervals, partly because I was so badly out of practice and partly because I couldn't keep my eyes from wandering to the back of Sam's head every few seconds.

Corrie could never understand what I saw in him. He was really quite average-looking, or at least that's what she said. To me he was the most beautiful thing I had seen, at least until I met Mitch and then each one of our children as they were born. Now as I stared at the back of his head, his broad shoulders and his arm as his hand flew swiftly and masterfully across his manuscript paper—I had to crane my neck a little to see that—all of those memories of him came spilling back. My palms were sweaty and I felt dizzy. Was I hyperventilating?

"Get a grip, Anne. He's a kid. He's seventeen years old, for heaven's sake," I whispered to myself under my breath.

"What did you say?" Corrie whispered back.

"Nothing." I waved her away and forced myself to ignore Sam and concentrate on the work. The lesson continued, and I was encouraged at how quickly the chord progressions and transposition came back to me. It brought a sense of satisfaction that I hadn't felt in a long time. By the end of the class time, I had actually written a short, two-stanza melody with a simple accompaniment. It was the first time in years I had created anything other than dinner or Halloween costumes for the kids, and it felt really good. It also gave me hope for my algebra test. If this came back that easily, then there was hope for me in math, I thought.

As Mr. Allan finished up his final notes, my stomach growled loudly, loud enough that the kids in front of me heard it and laughed.

"Good thing it's almost lunchtime," I said, trying to sound amused. It was embarrassing, though, mostly because I knew that twenty years ago I would have been embarrassed at anything that drew attention to the fact that I ate. A fat kid in high school isn't supposed to eat in front of other people. Ever.

The bell rang, and the others gathered their belongings and shuffled to the door. Corrie gestured for me to follow her, sensing that I needed the direction today, I guessed. I tried to hurry, but I wasn't as adept at shoving everything back into the severely overstuffed bag. *Did I really have to carry everything with me at all times?* I wondered.

When I straightened up, he was standing in front of me, and my heart stopped beating. I hadn't quite remembered his eyes. They were dark brown with thick lashes and strong eyebrows. They were intense. That was the defining characteristic of Sam. He was intense, and teenager or not, I was intensely attracted to him.

"We need to talk," he said seriously.

Shame washed over me as if I were a child caught by a parent in the act of breaking something important. Funny, though, I didn't remember seeing him today . . . twenty years ago. Had he missed school? Had I? Ah, that was probably it. I had skipped school, something that hadn't even occurred to me in this strange dream, despite my dad's earlier suggestion.

He waited for my answer, and I glanced at Corrie over his shoulder. She was grinning and giving me the thumbs-up sign, obviously thinking that this was a real breakthrough for me. I almost wished I had told her about my little fiasco of the day before so that she would understand that this wasn't going to be pretty. I looked back at him, forcing myself to focus on his face, and nodded.

He led me into Mr. Allan's office, a place where we all frequently hung out. There were a couple of other kids in there on a couch in the corner, sophomores just digging their lunches out of their backpacks, but Sam, with the power of his senior status, just pointed to the door and they scrambled to their feet and out the door. He closed it softly behind us. I was completely intimidated.

I'm thirty-eight years old. I have three kids and a mortgage and a dead husband whom I miss more than I can possibly express. I am not intimidated by a seventeen-year-old kid I'm never going to see after I get married, I thought.

"I'm actually eighteen. Last week," Sam said as he passed me to sit down on the couch.

My jaw dropped open. Had I actually said that out loud? Did it really matter? This was a dream. I was more sure of that fact than I had been before. This was the most dreamlike part of my day so far.

I stared at him, allowing myself to drink in the sight of his broad chest and deep brown eyes while I considered my options.

Okay, I thought, careful to keep silent this time, *if this is a dream, then it must be my subconscious trying to tell me something or work through an unresolved problem.* I thought about the conversation with my mother in the car. I had told her how sorry I was for hurting her, something I hadn't done in reality, and it had felt really good. Now I was faced with another opportunity to right a wrong. This must be what my dream was for. Making the connection took a lot of weight off my mind. I knew what I had to do. I followed Sam, feeling a little more confident, and sat down on the opposite end of the couch, as far away as the cushions would permit.

"Look, Sam, I owe you an apology. We were friends . . . sort of . . . and you always knew that I had a huge crush on you, practically since I was twelve. There's no way you couldn't know it. I mean, could I have been more obvious?" I laughed, a short sarcastic sound, and then cleared my throat to continue.

"It was just a teenage crush, though. Still, I know that it had to be pretty disturbing to have some girl threatening to kill herself and laying the responsibility on you. That wasn't fair, and I don't know what I was thinking. I guess we could chalk it up to immaturity and a desperate plea for attention."

This was horrible. Had I thought I could explain this in a way that would make sense? I soldiered on, just needing to be done with it.

"Really, though, it's not your fault, and I was never in danger of actually committing suicide. In fact, I have lived a very happy life without you, and I wish the same for you. You are a very nice boy, and I'm sure you are going to have great success in the Air Force and meet someone great and have some kids, and that will be that. So please don't worry about me. I'm just fine. I won't chase after you or write you letters or drive by your house on the way home from the store or call and hang up when you answer or any of that other bizarre teenage girl behavior anymore. You have my word."

That should do it. I had closure now, right? I was ready to wake up.

I closed my eyes and tried to picture myself waking up on The Rack in my thirty-eight-year-old body, complete with lines on my face and a few stray gray hairs that I had missed in my last hunt-and-pluck session. The room was completely quiet. I opened my eyes, and Sam was staring at me with a half grin on his face.

"Now, really, was that so bad?" he asked.

"What?" I asked.

"Just telling me how you feel? I mean, I'm not sure what all that other stuff was, but I got this much: You like me, right?" His eyes were doing that thing again, where they seemed to be trying to bore into my soul. It was that look that had kept me wrapped up in him for all those years.

"Liked. As in past tense." That was such an understatement it was almost comical. "Actually, I spent my entire life as a teenager, right up until I met Mitch, obsessing over you. And you spent all your time dating my friends and even making out with them right in front of me, and I put up with it because I was too in love with you to do anything different." Years' worth of anger was starting to boil beneath the surface. I paced back and forth, too fired up to be still.

"Meanwhile, I was the one that you called when you broke up with your girlfriend or needed to talk about your jerk of a stepfather or were just plain bored, and I sucked up every ounce of attention that you saw fit to bestow on me, hoping that it really meant that you loved me back instead of just thinking I was the fat freak who had a crush on you. It's twisted, and I'm not doing it anymore!"

I turned to storm out of the office, feeling powerful to have finally said all of that stuff to him. Now *that* was closure. He was right behind me, reaching out to grab my arm. The thrill that the simple touch sent through me made me mad.

"Wait. Who is Mitch?" he asked, spinning me around to face him. He was only inches away. I could smell the fabric softener in his shirt and see every individual eyelash around those amazing eyes. My bones felt like they would melt in the electric current that ran through me again, and I wondered if he felt it, too. I shoved that away, reminding myself that he was eighteen and I was thirty-eight and being attracted to someone half my age was definitely *not* okay. I forced myself to focus on his words instead of his hand.

"You must really have selective hearing if that is the only thing you got out of what I just said." I debated telling him that Mitch was my dead husband but that just sounded like another attention-getting device coming from the mouth of a sixteen-year-old. "Mitch is the man I'm going to marry in four more years, and you are the guy I'm never going to see again and whom I refuse to regret. I'm sorry again for any pain I might have caused you, but I'm not playing the game anymore, so you'll have to find someone else to be your ego booster."

His eyebrows were raised in surprise. I stared him down until he let go of my arm, and then I turned and walked purposefully out of the band room.

I got all the way to the hall before I realized what I had just done. I had stood up for myself to Sam, told him that I wouldn't be used to stoke the fire of his ego. The woman inside me applauded the brave move. Another part of my brain screamed at me, however, saying that what I had really done was tell him that I was in love with him and that I didn't want anything to do with him ever again—two contradictory things that were both strictly taboo for my teenage self to even think of mentioning, let alone say out loud.

The emotions that had been so close to the surface since I entered this crazy dream threatened to overwhelm me. I had the urge to laugh and to cry and to scream all at the same time. I had forgotten how extreme everything felt as a teenager. I ran to the nearest girls' restroom, pushing past a couple of frizzy cheerleaders and a punk wearing striped tights and green hair, and made it to the last stall before the tears came. It was like déjà vu . . . on steroids. This restroom. This stall. These tears. That guy. Wow, I had regressed twenty years. I desperately wanted to wake up. To get back to my real life, to see my children. But even as that thought came, another followed quickly behind it. *Other than your children, what do you have that's worth returning for?*

I had no real friends. I'd given up all of my hobbies, hadn't composed anything or played the piano or sung in years. My relationships with my parents and siblings, especially Hannah, were strained at best. I was a shell of a woman. What kind of mother could I be when I wasn't even a person anymore? I cried harder as I thought of the look on Mallory's face when she had hugged me good-bye. It was weary. It was worried. But it wasn't surprised. I had thought I'd hidden my grief so well, buried it so deep that it couldn't hurt them, yet she had looked as if she had been expecting this all along. Was that the way an eleven-year-old should be thinking? I was failing them. I needed Mitch in that moment so badly it seemed impossible that he could be dead. How could my need be so big without his being there to fill it, just as he had filled every other need of mine for the past thirteen years?

I wanted to wake up, but I was starting to suspect I wasn't dreaming at all. How could everything be so real? So detailed? My normal dreams didn't act like this. They jumped ahead in fits and starts with huge holes and odd little coincidences that didn't make sense. If I were dreaming, I would have encountered people from other stages of my life. My siblings would have been the wrong age, or Shelley Inger would have appeared as one of my teachers. Mitch would have been here, as he was in all of my dreams.

My tears dried up suddenly, and I gasped as a new thought bloomed. I leaned against the wall of the stall, and my mouth hung open as joy burst through every fiber of my being. Even if this wasn't real, if it was just a dream with me as a sixteen-year-old, then that meant Mitch was living on the other side of town, working and saving for college and living his life. Mitch wasn't dead. He couldn't be. We hadn't even met yet!

Chapter
6

I was twenty and Mitch was twenty-seven when we met at the local college. He was the older, more intelligent man who stood head and shoulders, literally, above all the boys in my classes. It wasn't just his height or his age or his brains that attracted me. He cared about people. Everyone else was still stuck in teenage drama, just a step away from high school in both age and maturity. He was an actual grownup who saw that people needed each other and needed to be cared for. I saw all of that before I even noticed that he was possibly the worst dresser I'd ever encountered and was also painfully shy. Everything he did was in the background—cleaning up a classroom when he left it, even though the garbage belonged to everyone else, helping people clear their cars of snow in that stormy January, offering to carry bags for someone on crutches. Someone like me.

I'd noticed him in the background, never really saying much unless he was especially passionate on a topic, but we'd never actually spoken until the day that he noticed me struggling to carry my bag into the building while limping on one crutch after ankle surgery. The strap kept falling off my shoulder, and the heavy bag threatened to knock my crutch right out from under me. It was my first day back, and I was already dreading the wrestling match my bag and I were going to experience throughout the long day ahead. Mitch was walking in at the same time and hurried to take my bag for me. When he was helping someone, his shyness faded away and his smile was beautiful. He walked with me to my first class, and we made small talk about school. He had noticed that we had American Lit together. I was flattered that he'd noticed. I found myself trying to tease him to keep that smile on his face. We said good-bye at the door, and I hoped to see him the next day. I was pleasantly surprised when he was waiting for me after class.

For the next three weeks he walked me to every single class and carried my books for me. It was delightfully old-fashioned and charming, and I stopped noticing that he was wearing clothes in patterns and colors that should never be combined. I stopped thinking of him as shy by the third day. I spent far too much time in class thinking of things that I could say to keep him smiling. The first day I came to school without my crutches, now in a walking splint, I was worried. Maybe he wouldn't see the need to help me anymore and our time together would be over. He had been waiting for me in his usual spot, and when I got out of the car and walked toward him without a crutch, he gave me a big thumbs-up sign. He reached for my bag and carried it even though I was capable of doing it.

When we had been going through that routine for nearly a month and he hadn't asked me out, I started to feel discouraged. The extent of my experience with boys was my experience with Sam, and that had never given me reason to think I was worth dating. Now, for the first time in my life, I was attracted to someone new, and he didn't seem to want to ask me out either. I got more depressed as each day went by. Mitch noticed the change. Finally he asked me what was wrong and— in another first for me—I told him.

"Mitch, every day you walk me to all of my classes. We joke and have great conversations, but that's as far as it goes. I'm just feeling down because I keep hoping you'll ask me out, yet day after day you say good-bye and that's it."

It took a lot of courage for me to be able to say that to him. I waited for him to shift his eyes away, make an excuse, and bolt, and I'd never see him again. Instead he smiled that beautiful smile of his.

"Annie, do you want to go out to dinner tonight?"

We went out that night, and the next day as he walked me to class, I built up enough courage to reach out and take his hand. I never let go of it for thirteen years.

Now, as I left the restroom and hurried to find Corrie, I recalled the conversation I'd had with Mitch that first evening. He had told me about his mission to Chile and how he'd gone back later with a group of friends on a service trip. He had come home on November 18th.

Corrie was just leaving the lunchroom when I caught up with her. She was in a crowd of other kids I knew I was supposed to recognize.

"Hi, guys," I said. Maybe they wouldn't realize I couldn't remember their names. "I need to steal Corrie for a minute, okay?"

A couple of them shrugged, and they all drifted away. Corrie was instantly a captive audience.

"What happened with Sam?" she asked breathlessly.

"Never mind that." I waved my hand dismissively in the direction of the band room. "What's today?"

"Uh, Monday. Seriously, though, what did he want to say to you? He looked all serious and stuff. It had to be good." I grabbed her arm and led her to the side of the hall, out of the way of the clusters of students drifting out of the cafeteria.

"What's the date?"

"The eighteenth. Did he ask you out? What did you say?" she begged.

"What is the month, Corrie? Please!" This could be the best day of my life.

"Annie. That's not fair. You have to tell me what happened." She started to pout.

"Okay. I'll tell you, but first, is it November?" I asked.

"Yes, duh! It's November. Now tell me!" She planted her hands on her hips and stood there looking as dangerous as someone that small could possibly manage.

My head was spinning. Mitch was getting home sometime today. His family would have a big homecoming party to celebrate, and I could see him. Today.

"I've got to go home," I said. I turned toward the front doors, but Corrie caught up with me.

"You can't just leave. If you cut one more day this year, you are going to be in so much trouble. Come on, Annie. If you get grounded, then we can't go to Girls' Choice, and my dad won't let me go unless we double. He still hasn't forgiven Jesse for bringing me home late last week." She was surprisingly strong for someone so tiny. Girls' Choice. Junior year. Another piece of information clicked into place, and I groaned and stopped walking.

"Jesse? As in Jesse Lingstrom?"

"What other Jesse could there possibly be?" She rolled her eyes.

"You're not dating him again? He's a complete scumbag," I said, but her face hardened into that stubborn Corrie face that brought back so many memories.

"Don't you dare, Annie. You are the only sane voice in my life. Don't start talking like my parents. There's nothing wrong with Jesse. I'm going to marry him someday," she said, her arms folded over her chest.

I thought about Mitch, alive and warm and just a few miles away, and then I looked at Corrie, headed for a serious problem with an abusive jerk. I was torn, but it was just a slight delay. Mitch would still be there after school, but if I left now, Corrie was right, I would be grounded. I had to hold back a laugh at the thought. Who knew what would happen in the next few days, or few hours, for that matter. Was I even really here? All I knew was that I had a choice to make, and I wasn't going to leave Corrie defenseless.

"Okay. I'll stay, but we have to talk about Jesse at some point."

She shrugged but didn't say no. It was a step in the right direction.

"You still have to tell me what happened with Sam," she said.

"Oh, yeah. I told him to find someone else to be his ego booster and not to talk to me anymore."

Corrie's jaw dropped, and then she started talking a mile a minute, but her words were lost in the roar of the bell ringing and kids pouring out of the cafeteria to their fifth-period classes. I grabbed her hand and pulled her toward our next class. A Cappella Choir was one thing I had never forgotten. I didn't even care that Sam would be there.

It wasn't until we were halfway through fifth period that I realized I'd still not studied for my algebra test. I looked with longing at my precious music folder and reluctantly dug my math book out of my bag and tried to hide it under the sheet music I was holding. But I had no idea what unit to look at. Corrie glanced over at me from the sopranos' side of the room and could see my panicked expression. She tried to mouth something to me a couple of times, but I couldn't tell what she was saying. She finally pulled out a piece of paper and scribbled something quickly, folded it, and asked her neighbor to pass it down. While we continued singing, I watched out of the corner of my eye as the note traveled along the row of sopranos. It would have reached me in seconds if it weren't for the immature tenors sitting in the middle.

The first boy—I thought his name was Tom or Tim or Troy— pulled out a pencil and scribbled something on the front of the folded paper, then handed it to his neighbor, a pimply, scrawny kid who had obviously not hit his growth spurt yet. The pimply kid followed Troy's example and then passed it on. Each of the boys followed Tim's example, slowing the note's progress to a snail's pace. I looked to the front of the room nervously as the note made its way into Sam's hands. Miss Lund's eyes were following the note, too. Her lips tightened, and she cut the choir off with a slicing motion.

"Would the tenor section care to join us today?" she asked sarcastically.

Sam was stuck holding the crumpled-up note and a pencil, which he tried to hide by stuffing them into his pocket. Miss Lund held out her hand in a wordless command, and Sam slowly obeyed, pulling the note out and handing it to her. I groaned silently. Miss Lund didn't even glance at it, just tossed it onto the piano behind her and returned her attention to the music.

"Women, at pickup to measure fifty-nine, please," she stated and then counted off the beats.

We resumed singing. "When Allen a Dale went a-hunting, his bow was stout and strong . . ." *Maybe I should ask to go to the nurse's office. I could lie down and skim through my textbook*, I thought. But I couldn't really force myself to care more about the math test than I did about singing tight harmonies and trilling cadences. Well, as much as altos were ever allowed to trill.

I put my algebra book back in my bag and focused on the music, allowing myself to be lost in the old-fashioned tunes and melodies as easily as the more modern arrangements. My soul drank in the music, and it flooded through me, hydrating the dried and cracked places in my spirit that had been thirsting for creation. Class ended much too soon. I could have sung for hours still, and I was brought back to the moment I'd been dreading. It was time for Algebra.

As I lugged my heavy bag back onto my shoulder—I really needed to start using my locker—it came to me that this was how I'd felt through high school the first time I'd lived it. I had loved every one of my music classes with a passion that was surpassed only by my interest in Sam, but I'd dreaded my math classes just as passionately.

I sighed and headed slowly out of the room to meet my fate. I wasn't going to fool myself into thinking that anything I had learned in the last twenty years was going to help me with algebra. Even helping Mallory with her homework had become an exercise in frustration for both of us over the last year. If I couldn't figure out sixth-grade math, then I had no hope of passing this test.

Someone bumped me from behind as I turned the corner to go to the stairs, and I nearly lost my balance. A couple of items spilled out of my bag and I bent to gather them up. Extra hands were there, gathering the papers and pens that had scattered farther than the rest. Sam straightened everything into a neat pile and handed it to me, the note from choir class balanced on top of everything else. I grabbed the things from him without meeting his eyes and shoved them back into my bag. I could feel his eyes on me as I started to climb the stairs.

Chapter
7

*I*t was horrible, Corrie," I groaned as we trudged out to the parking lot after school. "I didn't recognize anything. How on earth are you supposed to remember all of those formulas? Seriously, no one ever uses this stuff in real life after school. It's just a joke."

Corrie was going to give me a ride home. I had forgotten that she had a car.

"It wasn't that bad. We went over it all on Saturday. I can't believe you forgot it all already," Corrie said.

I laughed, wondering what she'd say if I told her that twenty years had lapsed since our study session. She went on. "At least it was an odd day, though, right? I won't even see you tomorrow, other than in orchestra. By the way, what did Sam write on that note? I saw him give it to you in the hall."

"Oh yeah. I forgot about that. I don't know. I don't plan on reading it. I'm through with him," I said. Corrie looked like she was about to start in on me again, so I hurried to change the subject. "My mom is going to freak out about that test. I hope I at least pass, or I'll have to have her sign it."

"Have your dad do it," Corrie said as she unlocked the door.

I reached for the handle but stopped when I heard a horn honk in the shave-and-a-haircut rhythm that our family always used for everything from knocking on doors to honking to get someone's attention. I looked up and saw the blue station wagon parked in front of the school and my mom waving to me urgently.

"I thought she wasn't picking you up today," Corrie said.

"I told her I was going to walk. Huh. Oh, well. I guess I'll see you tomorrow," I said as I moved toward my mom's car. I waved over my shoulder in response to Corrie's reminder to call her, but I was already wondering what had my mom looking so hurried.

"Hey, Mom. You didn't need to pick me up. I told you I was going to walk," I said as I opened the door and climbed in.

"Riding with the Crump girl is hardly walking," Mom said, her bluster back full force. "It doesn't matter. When I said you could walk home, it's because I forgot about your appointment with Dr. Santos. We have to hurry. We're going to barely make it in time." I held in a groan as I realized that it would be that much longer before I could get to Mitch's mother's house. Mom drove like a maniac, as usual, and I held on for dear life, dreading the speedily approaching appointment.

I hadn't met Dr. Santos yet, or at least the original sixteen-year-old me would have been meeting him for the first time today. When I had sat with my bishop on that horrible night, he had encouraged my parents to take me to a therapist to help me work through the depression I was obviously struggling with. He'd called his friend Dr. Santos at home and set up an appointment for the very next day. For the next six months, I was forced to travel weekly to his office and endure humiliating sessions as he tried to help me identify what had led me to want to kill myself. Somehow I had never managed to express to him that I hadn't really ever planned on doing it. He assumed that if I was depressed enough to write a suicide letter, then I was a danger to myself, no matter what I said. Finally, after six months my parents had run out of money (one more thing for me to feel guilty about), and the sessions had stopped. Now I was going to have to face it again.

Dr. Santos was a very small man with kindly eyes and a glistening bare scalp. He spoke with just a hint of a Portuguese accent that made his words sound musical. If I remembered correctly, one of the hardest things about therapy was trying to stay awake. He welcomed me into his office and encouraged Mom to make herself comfortable in the waiting room. I could tell that Mom thought she should come in with me, but I was relieved that Dr. Santos never even considered it. He directed me to a comfortable chair and pulled a matching one up so that he could sit facing me with our knees just inches apart. It was too close for comfort, and I scooted my chair back slightly. He smiled as he noticed the movement but didn't say anything about it.

"So, Miss May, can I call you Annabelle?" he asked.

"Annie," I replied, and he smiled and made a note in his file.

"Annie, then. Well, it's nice to meet you, Annie. As you know, I'm Dr. Santos. I want you to know what it is that I do. I am a psychologist, which means that I have a degree in psychology, and I specialize in working with youth. I am not a medical doctor, and I rarely use medications, unless absolutely necessary. Instead I try to focus on the understanding of human nature and emotional needs so that I can help you discover ways to overcome the challenges that you face. You aren't required to answer any questions that I ask, but answering them as truthfully as possible will help me to help you. Anything that you tell me will be kept strictly confidential, including from your parents, unless it involves breaking the law or puts someone, including yourself, in direct or immediate danger. Does that all make sense?"

I nodded, and he smiled again.

"I understand that you've been feeling a little depressed lately. Is that right?" he asked.

"No. I'm not depressed. I was just pulling a stupid stunt to try to get a boy's attention. He's not worth it, though, and I told him today that I'm not interested in continuing any sort of relationship with him." *There,* I thought, *that should do it. Maybe I'll be able to spare my parents the expense of all the therapy.*

Dr. Santos smiled at me and waited for me to say something else.

"Uh, so I don't really think that we need to continue this discussion, do we?" I asked.

Dr. Santos smiled again and pushed up his glasses.

"What is this boy's name?" he asked.

"It's Sam . . . wait, why are you writing that down? I'm not interested in Sam at all anymore. Trust me, that's over, so you don't need to worry about taking notes about him," I said, but he continued making a few scribbles on his notepad.

"Don't worry about these notes. They are just little things to help me to remember from week to week what we discuss. So, you spoke to him today? How did that go?" he asked, smiling. Did he never stop smiling?

"Fine," I said. I thought about telling him exactly what I'd said to Sam but figured that would get me locked up for sure. A little giggle escaped my lips at the image of Dr. Santos smiling and writing a note about the fact that I thought I was a thirty-eight-year-old widow and mother of three. The giggle caught his attention.

"What did you tell him?" he asked me.

"Well, like I said a minute ago, I basically said that he would have to find someone else to fawn over him. I wasn't going to do it anymore," I answered. Dr. Santos smiled. That was starting to irritate me.

"How did that feel?" he asked.

"Pretty great," I said, then I thought about how I had run to the restroom afterward and cried like a baby. "I guess I kind of hated it, too." Now I even sounded like a teenager. I felt like my adulthood was slipping away a little more with every minute I spent as a sixteen-year-old.

"Why did you hate it?" Dr. Santos asked me.

I had to think for a minute.

"I don't know exactly. Maybe it was the fact that I was letting go of my hopes that someday he'd fall in love with me. That was hard, I guess. I spent so many years obsessing over him, I guess it was just kind of pitiful that it never went anywhere. It just seemed like a waste." I knew that I was slipping back into speaking of my life in the past tense, and I tried to rein that in. "I mean, it *seems* like a waste."

"So you feel you are letting go of your hopes that Sam will fall in love with you. Is that right?" he asked. I recognized the reflective listening technique from the parenting books I'd read.

"Yes, basically. Still, I know there is someone better out there for me," I said. Yes, out there right now, while I'm stuck here talking to you about a boy who doesn't even matter. Dr. Santos made another little scribbled note.

"Annie, let me ask you this. Why did you write a suicide note and deliver it to Sam's house?" he asked bluntly, still smiling.

Darn, I thought. *I guess he was more informed than I'd thought.*

"Dr. Santos, let me ask you a question," I said. He nodded. "Is the main reason I'm here because my parents are worried I'm depressed, or is it because they think I'm going to harm myself?"

"Why do you think you're here?" he asked me evasively.

I groaned and threw my hands up. "Believe me, I really wish I could figure that one out," I said.

Chapter

8

*T*he rest of the session was pretty boring. I kept my answers short and tried to tell him what he wanted to hear, trying to remember how I would have answered as a teenager but still pulling hints from all those parenting books so that I could try to make him see that I really didn't need therapy. Still, the entire time we talked, his question rang in my head. *Why do you think you're here?*

I looked around at the stores and houses we passed as Mom drove back home, and I tried to find an answer to that question. Why was I here? Not just here, but *now?* Why was I living through this day as a sixteen-year-old? Was it so that I could right some wrongs with my mom or get closure with Sam? Was it to stop Corrie from the worst mistake of her life, or was it to see Mitch again?

We turned a corner, and suddenly there was the big white church. This was Mitch's home ward until we got married, and then we'd attended here during our first year of marriage. Memories flooded through me, and I gasped out loud.

"Mom, stop," I said. She glanced over at me and took in my stunned expression. They had torn down this church just a couple of years after we moved away—and there it was. I had to go inside. "Can we go inside the church, please, Mom?"

"Annie, I need to get dinner started," she said.

"I'll make dinner. Please?" I begged. She was going to pass it.

"You'll make dinner? Honestly, Annie," she laughed, but then she pulled over suddenly and parked in front of a blue house next to the church. It was Bishop Jamison's house. He had been bishop during the time we'd lived here. I didn't even wait for the car to come to a complete stop. I opened the door and stumbled out, walking quickly toward the church.

The doors were unlocked, and I went into the foyer, taking in the familiar smell of dust and old wood. The walls were hung with pictures of scenes from the scriptures and posters announcing a fall social for the ward. To the left was a large photo collage with pictures of different church activities, and I was drawn to it like a magnet. The pictures were new, but I remembered them with just a little bit more age to them. There was the photo in the bottom left corner that I knew I'd find. It showed a dozen or so young men and women with their suitcases on the day they were leaving for South America. In the back row, towering over everyone else, was a serious-looking young man with sandy blond hair and kind blue eyes. Mitch had pointed this picture out to me the first time we attended church together. He'd said that going back to Chile was one of the happiest times of his life, surpassed only by the day he met me. At that point the picture was four and a half years old; now it was barely a year old. The picture had disappeared years ago. Along with the church. Along with Mitch.

My mom was trying to decide if she should come after me or not when I got back to the car.

"What was that all about?" she asked, irritably.

"I, uh . . . I've just always loved that church, you know?" I said.

She made a noise in her throat but just drove off. I was more determined than ever to see Mitch.

"Mom, can I borrow the car tonight after dinner?" I asked after a few minutes.

"Don't you have homework?" she asked. Good question. I didn't know.

"I want to study with Corrie," I said, hoping that Corrie would be able to corroborate my story.

"Let's just get dinner done, and then we'll see, okay?" she said. I took a long look at her. She really was beautiful, but she was also very tired. With a start I realized that she was the same age as me. Well, as the real me. Was there something inherent in being a thirty-eight-year-old mother that made you worn out?

"Sure, Mom. I was serious about dinner, though. I can cook tonight," I said.

"Since when are you interested in cooking?" she asked.

"Hey, I'm probably more proficient than you think," I said. Mom was a great cook, but her style was simple, meat-and-potatoes cooking. I'd passed her up in variety and creativity ages ago. "Did you have something planned, or should I just wing it?"

Mom shot me another half-amused, half-annoyed glance.

"Well, if you're cooking, you can make whatever you want as long as we have the ingredients, I guess," she said. There was a hint of something in her voice that made me realize that she was just waiting to see what kind of mess I would make of dinner. I smirked a little to myself, thinking of her surprise when it turned out to be delicious.

Mom was surprised all right.

"Why are you getting out the ginger for a salad?" she asked me. "Honey, we use that to make cookies and pies. You're not going to want to put that on the chicken." She grabbed the little bottle of ground ginger to put it back in the spice cupboard.

"Mom, give that back. I need it. Trust me. This is going to be one of your favorite dishes someday. It's an Asian chicken salad. The ginger is to season the chicken and to go in the dressing."

Mom looked doubtfully at me but handed the jar back.

"Don't you need a recipe or something?" she asked.

"Trust me," I said again and shooed her out of the kitchen. It had been a while since I'd cooked enough food for this many people. My children weren't very big eaters, so it took a little longer than I expected to cut enough chicken for my parents' family into strips, and glaze it, and broil it, but the rest of the preparations were pretty quick. I had to improvise on a couple of the ingredients in the salad since my mom had never even heard of a dried cranberry, but I thought it all looked delicious.

And I was starving. I mean hungry in a way that made me surprised the entire world couldn't hear my stomach rumbling. I'd skipped breakfast and lunch, and it was obvious that my body was ready for food. Now.

"Dinner!" I called, and there was a stampede to the table. Dan was the first to arrive, and he immediately started picking chicken out of the salad until Mom smacked his hands away. He was distracted by Rachel, who insisted that he was sitting in her seat, and an argument ensued. Dad quietly took his place at the head of the table while Mom tried to break up the fight between her two youngest children. I sat down in my usual place, and finally Hannah arrived.

I hadn't seen her yet, and I stared in wonder at my sister as Mom tried to calm everyone down for grace. Hannah was very deliberately not looking at me. Her eyes were red rimmed and her jaw was clenched. What was up with her?

"Thanks to Annie for our dinner tonight. This is, uh, a real treat," Dad said, and I could tell he was as worried as Mom, just trying to put on more of a brave face. I smiled in reassurance, knowing they were going to love it. Dad said the prayer, and Mom started dishing salad onto plates and passing them around the table.

"Is there any ranch dressing?" Dan asked.

"You don't need it. It's already got the dressing on it. Just go ahead and try it," I said.

He eyed his portion warily, then poked it with a fork, sorting the lettuce from the chicken and the fruit.

"Mom, there are oranges in my salad," Rachel whispered.

Mom just shook her head and bravely picked up her fork. I watched as she took her first bite. Her face cleared, and a small smile appeared on her lips as she chewed.

"Mmmm, Annie. This is really good. What did you call it again?" she asked.

"It's Asian chicken salad. It's one of my favorite recipes," I said.

Hannah rolled her eyes next to me and muttered under her breath.

I thought I heard something like "show off," but I wasn't sure. Dad ate his salad and quietly asked questions of family members, inquiring into each one's day. I was too busy shoveling salad into my mouth to be interested in what everyone was doing. I was shocked to discover that I'd polished off mine before anyone else. I looked in the bowl. There was still enough for seconds for at least a couple of people, so I took a little bit more.

"Well, Annie. We're ready for the main dish, now, it looks like," Dad said.

I stopped chewing. Main dish? Surprisingly, it was Mom who jumped to my rescue.

"This is dinner tonight, family. So eat up. It's good for us to have more vegetables and eat a little lighter."

Dan groaned, Hannah glared, but Dad just smiled and took seconds. I was going to have to remember how to make heavier dishes if I was going to be staying here. That thought made me lose my appetite. I laid down my fork.

"Mom, did you think about my borrowing the car tonight?" I asked.

Mom didn't look up, just pushed her food around on her plate for a minute. You could feel the tension in the air, and Hannah looked up with interest.

"Annie, I don't think tonight is a good idea. Your father and I still haven't discussed what limits you'll be living under for the time being."

"Mom, please. Just for an hour? I'll be quick. I just really, really need to study with Corrie tonight. It's important," I begged, knowing I sounded far too desperate for the excuse I was using.

"What is so important that it can't wait?" Mom asked.

How could I answer that?

"Uh," I managed.

"If this is about that guy," Mom began, and I started, thinking of Mitch. "He's too old for you, and he's not interested, Annie. Can you understand that? Please?" Her voice was rising in volume and pitch.

"I'm sorry. Who are you talking about?" I asked, a knot in my stomach.

"Sam, Annie. Who else would I be talking about?"

Dad cleared his throat loudly and looked significantly at the other three children at the table. Mom got the hint.

"Annie, let's talk in my room," she said. It wasn't a request.

I glanced apologetically at Dad, and he mirrored my expression, winking at me. At least I had one ally. I got up and followed Mom out of the dining room and upstairs to my parents' room. She closed the door firmly behind me.

"Maybe this is way overdue, but we need to talk about girls and boys, Annie," she said.

I couldn't help it. The tension of the day, all of the crazy ups and downs, came crashing in as I realized that we were about to have The Talk. Again. I started laughing, and I couldn't stop.

"Annie, this isn't funny. It's just as uncomfortable for me as it is for you," Mom said.

"Mom," I gasped out. "You really don't have to do this. I promise." The look on her face was such a comical blend of worry, determination, and embarrassment that it set me off again. She tried to talk over the noise I was making.

"Well, when a boy and a girl really like each other, it is natural to want to . . . well, they sometimes feel like . . . well, boys can try to get you to . . . Annie! Can you please stop laughing, I can't hear myself think!"

"I'm sorry, Mom. It's just your face," I said, but I couldn't keep from laughing at her expression. She stared at me as I held my sides and collapsed onto her bed. A hint of a smile appeared at the corners of her mouth.

"Honestly, Annie. I just don't know what has gotten into you today," she said, trying to sound annoyed, but that smile was still there.

"I don't either, Mom," I said truthfully, my laughter calming into a chuckle. "I'll tell you this, though, being a teenager isn't at all how I remembered it."

"What?" she asked.

"What I mean is that it's harder than I thought it would be. Still, I get what you are trying to say. I need you to believe me that I'm not in danger of doing anything stupid with a boy. I'm saving myself for someone special," I told her. He's very special, I wanted to say. You are going to love him, more than you love me, I think, and he's going to take this crazy, overly emotional teenager and help her to become a mature and caring woman. I hope.

I don't know if it was the words I said or if maybe Mom could see a hint of the thoughts in my mind, but she sat down next to me and put her arms around me.

"Annie, you know I'm so hard on you just because I love you, right?" she said.

I hugged her back, breathing in that floral scent that always clung to her. In this moment there was no competition or confrontation. She was Mom, and she made me feel better.

"Thanks, Mom. I love you," I told her as she let me go. "I'd better go clean up dinner," I said, still kind of hoping that she'd let me use the car.

"It's Hannah's night for dishes," she said. Hope flared within me for a second. "Maybe you better get started on your homework." It died again.

"Yeah, okay. I'll, uh, be in my room," I said.

Chapter

9

I really didn't know if I had any homework or not, but I couldn't work in that disaster area anyway, so instead of doing homework I cleaned my room. The laundry was the biggest problem. I couldn't believe that there wasn't a single item of clothing in my dresser or my closet. It was all scattered on top of the dresser, on the chair, and, mostly, all over the floor. It took me about four loads of laundry to get it all clean. There was no way I could sleep, either, so I just stayed up waiting for the last load of laundry to dry. Meanwhile, I gathered up two garbage bags full of trash. It was telling how many candy wrappers I found.

While I worked, I listened to the radio. It was surreal hearing all of the old songs played as if they were new and fresh. George Michael, Roxette, and Sinead O'Connor all serenaded me with their outdated top-forty hits, and I sang along with them until it got too late for me to make that much noise. I passed Mom a couple of times in the hall on my way to the laundry room, and her face had that startled look I'd seen a lot that day.

"What are you doing?" she asked the first time.

"Cleaning my room. I have to do some laundry, or I'm not going to have anything to wear tomorrow," I said.

"Oh, okay," she answered, skeptically. "Do you want me to show you how to use the washing machine?" I laughed.

"No, I got it. Thanks, though." I left her with her jaw hanging open.

As I waited for the laundry, I sat down on my bed and pulled my school bag up in front of me. It was a miniature reflection of the chaos of my room, and I decided to tackle it as well. As I pulled out the trash—more candy wrappers—and organized everything, I found the note that Corrie had tried to pass to me during choir. I set it to the side as I continued to look for one specific piece of information that I had always scrawled inside a notebook at the beginning of the school year and then promptly ignored.

I found it in a red notebook—my locker number and combination. Yes! I wasn't going to be bound to this hideously heavy bag anymore.

When I had been sixteen—the first time—I had never used my locker because it meant extra trips up and down the stairs, and I wasn't exactly one for gratuitous physical exertion. But I wasn't going to be subjected to the back pain anymore. I'd rather run the stairs than lug this behemoth for one more day.

I took a shower, wanting things to be easier in the morning, especially considering my late night. As I got out and confronted my reflection, I didn't even care about the extra weight. Everything was so firm and, well, perky! I chuckled to myself as I pulled on a clean pair of pajamas and climbed into clean sheets.

I tried to get comfortable, tugging at the blankets and pillows, and my hand encountered a piece of paper. The note again. I felt like it was following me. I sighed in exasperation and sat up, flicked on my lamp, and took a good look.

My name was scrawled across the front of the folded paper, lacking the curls and bubbles that usually adorned Corrie's handwriting. She had been in a hurry. Surrounding my name were stupid comments by the boys in the choir. One boy had added a large capital M in front of my name and an L before the I, a lame pun to turn my name into Manly. Like I hadn't heard that one before. Another boy had drawn something crude involving two lizards. His artwork was actually pretty impressive. I ignored the other comments and opened the note. There was a simple scrawl inside. "Unit 17," it said, specifying the algebra unit. Too late. I folded the note back up and was about to toss it onto the nightstand when something caught my eye.

The back of the folded note had also been scribbled on. It was just one sentence: "Who is Mitch?"

That one was obviously Sam's. I groaned and threw it in the trash.

An hour later I was still awake. At first I didn't understand why my teenage body that so desperately needed rest wouldn't crash after a day like today, but the answer was glaringly obvious. I was afraid to fall asleep, afraid that I would wake up back in my real body and my real time, in a world where Mitch was dead. I missed my kids horribly, but I knew they were in the future somewhere if I stayed in this time, and, dream or not, I didn't want to leave Mitch behind.

The second reason I couldn't sleep was that I was hungry. My stomach was trying to gnaw through to my backbone. I needed food. I glanced at the clock: 1:30 a.m. The house had been quiet for hours now. I climbed out of bed and tiptoed downstairs to the kitchen, where I dug through the pantry and pulled out cocoa, powdered sugar, vanilla, and graham crackers and then butter and milk from the fridge. I should have eaten a piece of fruit or some cereal even, but this body wanted graham crackers and chocolate buttercream frosting, and I wasn't going to argue with it.

I was only a little surprised when I heard Dad's slightly uneven tread on the stairs.

"Hi, Dad. You want a snack?" I asked just before he came around the corner. He grinned at me.

"Can't fool you, can I, baby cakes?" he chuckled. "Can you set me up with a couple of those and some milk?"

"Sure, Dad," I said. I made a couple of frosting-and-graham-cracker sandwiches and put them on a second plate, poured another glass of milk, and carried them to the table. Dad picked up a cracker and dunked it in his milk, then bit off a huge piece and chewed with satisfaction.

"Mmmm. That sure hits the spot. Not that your salad wasn't quite tasty, but I could have used something with a little more oomph to it. Know what I mean?" he said.

"I know. I was thinking the same thing," I said with a quiet laugh. There was a peacefulness about Dad that kept our family from boiling over, and it permeated the kitchen at this moment, calming me and warming me all at the same time.

"So, you've been cleaning your room and making dinner, and I noticed you were real nice to your mother today. I think it's a good start, Annie Bell." He liked to make my name sound like two words. "'Today is the first day of the rest of your life,' and you made it a real good one."

I smiled and took another bite of my graham cracker sandwich. We munched contentedly for a few more minutes, and then Dad stretched and patted his stomach.

"Well, that was a great treat, Annie Bell, but it's late. You should probably get to bed. I'll clean up down here."

"It's okay, Dad. I can do it," I said, jumping up to clear the plates and glasses.

"What? You think a one-armed man can't do dishes?" he asked in mock offense.

I rolled my eyes at this familiar protest.

"'A one-armed man can do anything a two-armed man can do, single-handedly,'" I answered with his favorite line.

"That's right, and don't forget it. Now get to bed." He swatted me on the rear as I walked out of the kitchen.

"Good night, Dad," I said softly.

"Night, baby cakes," he called back.

I don't know if it was the food in my stomach or the time spent with Dad, but whatever the reason, I fell asleep the moment my head hit the pillow.

Chapter

10

The radio flicked on automatically at six a.m. Bon Jovi. What a way to wake up. My eyes flew open, and I jumped out of bed in excitement.

"I'm still here!" I shouted, punching a fist in the air. I danced through the morning as I got ready, actually going through the ritual of curling iron and hairspray this morning. I put together an extremely retro—to me—ensemble of jeans and a white blouse with a floral print vest and half boots. I giggled as I looked in the mirror.

"Annie, are you up?" Mom called, knocking on my door. I bounced over to open it.

"Come in, Mom," I said. "Isn't it a beautiful day?"

"Um, I guess," she said distractedly, looking around my room in amazement. "Your room looks really good, Annie. Can you try to keep it this way this time?" she asked.

"Sure, Mom. I'll try. What time do we need to leave?" I asked, dancing past her to gather my newly organized school bag. I'd examined my schedule last night and put everything in my bag in order so that I could put it in my locker and have the first class on the top of the pile. Today was going to be perfect.

"We still have about twenty minutes. You should eat some breakfast," she answered, looking at the clothes hanging neatly in my closet.

"Great idea! I'm starving!" I said. I kissed her on the cheek as I left the room and bounded down the stairs.

My sisters and brother were eating cereal.

"Good morning, guys. Did you sleep well?" I asked. Dan and Rachel ignored me completely, but Hannah glared.

"Why do you even care, lame-o," she grumbled.

"Well, dear sister, I care a great deal about your welfare. You are obviously angry at me about something, but I choose to ignore that and focus on the fact that we are young and alive and sisters, and, as such, we should be there to support each other in times of trouble as well as in times of peace. Can you please pass the cereal?"

Hannah's mouth was hanging open, and I smiled angelically at her. Nothing was going to ruin my day today.

By lunchtime I was no longer smiling.

I shoved my chemistry books into my locker roughly and slammed the metal door with a clang.

"What's the matter?" Corrie asked as she bounced to a stop beside me.

"High school is ridiculous," I said. "The amount of time spent dealing with bad behavior is grossly out of proportion to the time spent learning. A vast majority of the content is absolute drivel, and the teachers are prejudiced and simpleminded. How does anyone have the nerve to call this education?"

Corrie laughed and bounded toward the stairs. "Nice vocab jump, Annie. I'm taking it that Mrs. Crayk was being a bear again."

"That woman shouldn't be allowed around all these children. She's toxic. It's obvious that she has some serious personal issues causing her to treat everyone so poorly," I said. "Not to mention that Mr. Hanover is a lecher and spends more time looking at the girls' legs and down their shirts as he walks around the room than he does actually teaching anything remotely resembling chemistry. How did I put up with this before?"

"Before what?" Corrie asked, stopping on the stairs. I hurried to backpedal.

"Just, you know, before today," I said. I really needed to watch my words.

Corrie accepted my answer and ran quickly down the last few

stairs. "Well, at least you have orchestra next," she said, spinning around to wiggle her eyebrows at me in a suggestive manner.

I groaned. "I hope I can play the music. I haven't played in years," I muttered, forgetting my resolution of just moments before.

Corrie looked at me in confusion, but luckily our conversation was interrupted as we entered the cafeteria and moved to take our place in line for food. By the time we made our selections and found a table, Corrie seemed to have forgotten my last comment.

"Okay, so we have got to get things figured out for Girls' Choice. Have you asked him yet?" she asked with her mouth full. It was surprising how much food she could fit in her mouth.

"Uh, I don't know, Corrie. I'm not sure that a dance like that is such a great idea for me right now," I said.

Corrie dropped her pizza back onto her plate with a plop. "No way, Annie. You promised. I told you I can't go without you going, too. Don't do this to me! You just have to get up the guts and ask him already. It's only, what, three days away? If you don't hurry, that horrid Miranda is going to ask him, so no more excuses. Just get it done. You can do it next period." I started to protest, not needing to ask who "him" was supposed to be, but she cut me off. "No arguments! You owe me!"

I looked at her face and thought about my last memory of her after graduation. All the hope had gone out of that face, and the glow of health, too. It all started with Jesse and that dance. I hadn't ever gotten up the courage to ask Sam to the dance, and I hadn't wanted to go with anyone else, so she had gone on her own.

"Okay, okay. But I'm not asking Sam. I'll ask someone else." I continued eating as I tried to remember who else there was I could possibly ask. Corrie seemed skeptical, but she was no longer pouting. We ate quietly for a couple of minutes, and then Corrie looked up.

"What about Travis?" she suggested. Travis, Travis? I couldn't remember anyone by that name. I guess she could see the blank look on my face. "Duh, Travis, that kid who gave you and Hannah a ride home last week and then sat in your driveway for two hours talking. Seriously, Annie, how can you not remember that?"

"Uh, sorry. I guess I'm just brain dead today. I'll think about it. I'll figure something out."

"Well, you should definitely ask him. He was totally into you. I was going to suggest it before, but you're always so focused on, well, you know," she finished, her eyes drifting to the back corner of the cafeteria.

I followed her gaze to see Sam sitting with a couple of other seniors I probably should have recognized. He glanced up at me, and I quickly averted my gaze, hoping he hadn't caught me looking.

"Yeah, I know, but that is done. Over. Finished. I have officially come to my senses," I said. Corrie didn't seem to take me seriously. She just shrugged.

"Okay, whatever you say. Well, whoever you ask, you had better get it figured out right away. Like today." The bell rang, and we gathered up our trash, dumping it in the can on the way out the door.

"Well, good luck in orchestra," Corrie said.

"Thanks. I'll see you after school?" I asked. I had to ask her for a favor.

"Yeah." She walked away, and I watched her go, wondering if I could figure out a way to get her away from Jesse. Suddenly I felt a warm breath on the back of my neck as someone stood too close to me for comfort. I jerked and turned as I stepped away. Sam was standing there with a little smirk on his face.

"Did I startle you?" he asked.

I rolled my eyes and turned to go to class without answering.

"Wait, Annie. I'll walk with you," he said, hurrying to catch up.

I ignored him and kept walking, wondering why he couldn't just leave well enough alone. Hadn't I made myself perfectly clear yesterday? Even while I thought it, I still felt that thrill of electricity that seemed to buzz through me whenever I was anywhere near him. I was annoyed by that fact, and it made me walk faster.

"Where's the fire?" Sam quipped as he lengthened his pace to keep up easily with me.

"I'm just in a hurry to be away from you," I blurted, rudely.

"That's going to be a little bit difficult considering that we are going to the same class, don't you think?" he asked with a grin on his face.

"Blast. I forgot about that," I said, coming to a halt. The details were coming back to me now—me at the piano and Sam sitting no more than ten feet away playing the cello, a constant fight to make myself look at my music more than I looked at him, a feeling of inadequacy in knowing that he could play the piano part better in his sleep, and all of it wrapped up in the awkward environment of a barely more than mediocre high school orchestra.

"Annie, what's up with you lately?" he asked, his calm exterior finally cracking a little bit as he moved to stand in front of me with his arms crossed, as if to block my path. "You're giving me that note one minute, totally freaking me out, and then the next you are telling me you're married and don't want ever to see me again. To be honest, it's a little hard to follow. Can you please just help me understand?"

"Listen, Sam, I really am sorry about that whole, you know, suicide thing on Sunday. I can't do more than apologize, which I've done twice now. It was completely unfair to push all that emotional baggage onto you as if it were your fault. It makes me sick to think of what that could do to a person, but trust me, it's better if we just don't associate with each other anymore. We have some classes together . . ."

"And church," he interrupted.

"Right, and church, but . . ."

"And performances and sectionals," he added.

"Okay, classes and church and performances, but that doesn't mean . . ."

"What about the musical? Are you going to audition?" he asked.

I threw up my hands and sighed.

"I don't know! Look, I'm trying to make this easier on both of us. So we are thrown together a lot, so what! Does that mean that we have to continue this . . . this sick twisted thing that keeps dragging on and on? No!" I pushed past him and kept walking, mumbling to myself now. "You know, that was always the problem. I couldn't ever get over you because I saw you so much, every single stinking day, and there you were, sitting there looking all intense and brooding like you had some deep mystery to be unraveled, and I was totally sucked in. Add to it the fact that you pulled stunts like this all the time, cornering me and trying to make me feel like it was really important to you whether I lived or died. It worked, okay? I cared! I cared so much that I had myself tied up in knots for years wondering if you really loved me secretly and maybe there was just something mysterious holding you back." Oh, how true that had been.

I spun back to face him. "Believe me, I had a very vivid imagination, and it kept me hoping. And just when I'd get sick of the whole game and decide that I was done with waiting around for you, you'd call me and tell me how much our conversations helped you and how you couldn't make it through all the garbage with your family without me, and I'd feel all validated and important and then I'd show up to school the next day expecting there to be something new and significant between us, and you'd be there, flirting with Jane or Miranda and acting like we were barely acquaintances." The hurt and hopelessness I'd felt were surprisingly fresh in my mind. "You know," I said, advancing toward him, "it's a miracle that I was ever able to actually trust Mitch enough to let myself be vulnerable with him in the first place."

He stepped back at the expression on my face.

There was a spark of anger in his response. "There's that name again. Annie, wait! Who in the world is Mitch?" he asked, jumping in front of me again as I turned to stride away, his eyes boring down into mine. "And before you say that whole thing about selective hearing again, yes, I heard what you said. I don't get it, but I heard it. Seriously, though, I don't even know anyone named Jane, and I'm definitely not interested in Miranda. I've never flirted with anyone in front of you or dated any of your friends."

"Oh, yeah? Well, you will. Just wait a month or two." The impossibility of this conversation washed over me, leaving me drained of my anger. I swiped a hand through my hair.

"Look, I've had a really bad day, and I can't even express to you how bad the last couple of years have been, so I'm really not in the mood to play this game again with you. Just trust me. I don't want to do it anymore. Go live your life. I'm going to live mine, and you aren't in it." I waited for him to move, trying to stare him down. He didn't move.

"Please, Sam? Please?" I said quietly, suddenly feeling very close to tears. Curse these stupid teenage emotions. He paused just a minute longer and then stepped aside.

"He's a lucky guy, you know," he said quietly as I reached for the doorknob.

"Who is?"

"This Mitch person. I hope he doesn't hurt you. You deserve something really wonderful," he said as he turned and walked in the other direction. That's when the teenage emotions won out again, and I ended up back in the same stall in the same restroom as the day before, crying and sniffing my way through half a roll of toilet paper.

Stupid Sam, who acted like he cared when he obviously didn't. Stupid Mitch for leaving me. Oh, yes, he had definitely hurt me, obviously not on purpose, but, still, it hurt all right. Stupid me for allowing that stupid teenage boy get to me. Stupid school for existing in the first place. Stupid restroom for not having an actual box of tissues. Stupid toilet paper for making my nose raw. Stupid, stupid, stupid.

$\mathcal{M}$itch was an accounting major, which meant he had to go to the same amount of schooling as a lawyer but ended up getting paid a lot less. We were married during my junior year as a music performance major. It was his senior year, and we decided it would be best for me to work for a few years while he finished up his degrees, and then he would be able to support me through the rest of my education before we would have children.

I was happy to do it, even though I was excited to have a family. I knew that waiting a few years would make things so much easier in the long run. I worked at a music store in the mornings and taught voice and piano lessons in the afternoons for a couple of years, leaving my evenings free for me to participate in local theater performances. He came to my practices and worked on his homework while he listened to me sing, and then we'd snatch a late dinner somewhere on the way home. It was a wonderful time.

Eventually, though, our expenses outstripped the tiny income I was bringing in, and Mitch decided he'd quit school and go to work to support us. I couldn't bear for him to quit when he was so close to his master's degree, so, without consulting him, I took an evening job working as a front desk clerk at a hotel. That left no time for performances. The grueling schedule started to wear on me, leaving me horribly exhausted, and I finally let the music lessons go. They weren't paying the bills anyway. That's about when the nausea hit, and the job at the music store disappeared next, to make way for my mornings spent throwing up. And thus my life of music was quickly replaced by life as a mother. I never went back to school.

Mitch always felt guilty about it. Our five-year plan hadn't worked at all. He would encourage me to sing whenever I could, which translated into performing solos with the church choir and playing piano for the occasional wedding or funeral, but I didn't really notice the lack. I was so happy to have my family and felt that the greatest use for my voice was singing lullabies to my babies. I didn't allow myself to regret not having music in my life, but somewhere inside something was slowly shriveling up and dying.

Now as I sat at the piano, clumsily trying to pick up the simple chording of one of the Brandenburg concertos, that shriveled-up part of my heart started to wriggle and expand. It had started the day before in Music Theory and increased in A Cappella Choir, but today it burst suddenly into bloom. I thought of all the years I had ignored this part of my life and realized sadly that I had yet another loss to mourn.

"Again at fifty-four, please," Mr. Allan cued, and I scanned the music to find the correct starting measure. As I looked back up to watch for the downbeat, my eyes skimmed past the empty chair in the cello section. Sam hadn't come to class.

For the rest of the class time I had to fight the distraction that empty chair created. As I stumbled through the concerto, I wondered why I never had found the guts to break away from Sam during my first try at being a teenager. When I embarrassed myself severely in a Tchaikovsky piece by not managing to find even the right key, I was wondering why he had left, why he couldn't seem to accept that I wasn't interested. Finally, when Mr. Allan suggested that we split up into sectionals, with an exasperated look in my direction, I was free to ponder the biggest question of all. Why did I even care?

With a start, I realized that I'd spent just as much time thinking about Sam today as I had about Mitch. My stomach clenched at the thought.

When class time ended, I gathered up my things and headed for the door.

"Annie, may I speak with you?" Mr. Allan called from the front of the room. I winced but followed as he gestured me toward his office.

"So, Annie, I noticed you were struggling today," he said.

"Um, yeah. Sorry," I said.

"And I was looking at your work from class yesterday. It seems you are getting a little lazy. This composition is far more simplistic and formulaic than I would have expected from you." I started to respond, but he interrupted me. "Now, don't worry, I know you have the work in you. You just need to apply yourself a little more, Annie. Music is something that comes naturally to you, and it's easy to rest on your laurels, to not really try. I expect more out of you because I know you are capable of more. So this is what I'd like you to do." He rummaged through a few papers on his desk and pulled out a large manila envelope and handed it to me.

"This is a cello sonata that I want you and Sam to play together for our Winterfest concert in a couple of weeks. It has a lovely, lyrical piano part that would really suit your abilities, and it would definitely show you both off."

I started to protest before I even looked at the music, but he cut me off.

"Now, look. I know you are a junior and primarily a vocalist, but it's never too early to be thinking about ways to improve your scholarship chances. Still, this isn't really about you. Sam is a senior, and he needs this. Our music program in this school is not meeting his needs. You could really help him out. Please, at least make a go of it. He lives near you, right?" Mr. Allan asked.

"Yes. A couple blocks away," I answered, a sinking feeling in my stomach.

"Great. Maybe you could drop off his copy, too? Even start working on it before Thursday?" He took my silence as acquiescence. "Good! Well, you'd better hurry for your next class. Thanks, Annie."

I took the envelope and stuffed it in with the other music I was taking home to work on before the next class time. As I walked to my

German class, I wondered why this was happening to me. I had never played a duet with Sam in school the first time around. What had changed?

Herr Dieter had to call my name several times to answer his question, but I didn't know the answer anyway. I had retained virtually no German, and my mind was completely caught up in a sickening thought that had occurred to me after talking to Mr. Allan.

What if I was messing things up? What if this was real and I was seriously going to be living my life again but something that I had done was going to change the future? Would I end up with Mitch at all? What about my kids? If the duet was new, and I was debating changing Corrie's future, what about mine?

While I found it hard to believe that I was actually here, actually living this life, I still found myself getting more and more ill as the class period dragged on and on. The faces of my children danced before me—James with his chubby baby cheeks and cute little giggle, Jenna with her funny way of phrasing things and her love of reading, and Mallory. Tender, nurturing Mallory, who worried way too much about me and seemed to carry the weight of the world on her slim shoulders. Was I taking away their chance to live their lives because I was trying too hard to change my own?

My mind went around and around in circles, looking for answers where none existed. Only one thought kept returning: I need to see Mitch. Today.

When the bell rang, I bolted for the door, desperate to get to Corrie.

I beat her to her car and waited impatiently as I watched the other students pouring out of the school. They were just children. I felt so out of place suddenly. What had I been doing these past two days, pretending to be a teenager?

Finally Corrie skipped toward me.

"So? Did you ask him?" she asked.

"Uh, ask who what?"

"Ask Travis to Girls' Choice? Or did you change your mind and ask Sam after all?"

"I'm not taking Sam," I said, wondering when I was supposed to have asked Travis. Had I seen him today? It didn't matter. "Corrie, I need you to do me a favor. Can you give me a ride? I really need to, um, see something, and my mom won't let me take the car. Please?"

"Where?" I gave her Mitch's mother's address. "That's clear on the other side of town, Annie. What is it that you need to see?" She climbed into the car, and I followed suit.

"It's complicated. But it's really important. Please? I'll be your slave for life if you'll help me out," I begged.

Corrie rolled her eyes and laughed. "Yeah, like I haven't heard that before. Seriously, though, I don't think I can today. I have so much homework, and if I don't get my composition done by tomorrow, Mr. Allan is going to kill me. Oh, I meant to ask you, did Mrs. Crayk assign your class that paper where you have to interview someone interesting and write an article? I have no idea who to choose. Anyway, it's Tuesday. Don't you have some church thing you have to go to?"

I started to ask her what church thing she was referring to, but my words were cut off as she accelerated quickly out of the parking lot. I glanced back toward the school just in time to see Hannah watching a tall, black-haired boy I thought I'd seen in German class getting into his car. I couldn't tell for sure from that distance, but it looked like she might be crying.

"Hey, wait, Corrie. Let's see if Hannah needs a ride."

Corrie eyed me skeptically but slowed down and pulled over.

I rolled down the window and waved my arm, calling across the parking lot. "Hannah, over here. Do you want a ride home?" Hannah whirled around to face me and then glanced back quickly as the black-haired boy pulled out of the parking lot.

She turned back. "Get away from me!" she screamed, and it was obvious that she really was crying. Then she turned on her heel and darted away. I was stunned. I sat back in the car as Corrie pulled out into traffic and headed home.

"I don't know why you even bother, Annie," she said.

"I wonder why she was crying. Who was that boy anyway?" I asked.

"Which one?"

"The tall one. She was looking at him and crying."

"I don't know. I didn't see anyone," she said.

I worked it over in my mind as we made the short drive home. Corrie chatted easily, not really caring if I responded to any specifics as long as I made the appropriate listening noises. What was eating at Hannah? We'd never been really close, but I didn't remember our really hating each other. Had I changed something, or was I just noticing it for the first time, sensitive to things in a way I hadn't been as a teenager? I had to find out. Maybe there was something there that could be fixed. Even as I thought it, though, I worried what more change now would mean for my future.

Chapter

12

inner was sedate. Hannah wasn't speaking to me, it seemed, and her eyes were red rimmed, but Mom was in a surprisingly good mood and had even taken the time to make homemade chicken pot pie, one of my favorite dishes and something we rarely ate on a weeknight. It was a little sad to realize how the clearest memories of my childhood seemed to involve food.

Dad was obviously grateful for the hearty meal and entertained us all with his favorite one-armed man jokes.

"Dan, here's one for you. How do you get a one-armed man out of a tree?" Dad asked.

"Duh, Dad." Dan rolled his eyes but couldn't help the smile that was twitching on his lips. Rachel waved her hand.

"I know, I know. You wave at him. Right?" she said. Dad frowned in mock severity.

"I guess I've told that one before. I've got a new one, though. You've never heard it before this," he said. "Why did the one-armed man cross the street?" he asked, glancing around the table. Mom just smiled. Dan and Rachel stopped eating and looked confused. Hannah ignored us, as usual.

"I knew it! You haven't heard it. Well, I'll tell you . . ."

"Come on, guys, you know this one. To get to the secondhand shop," I said, laughing. "It's a classic." Dad groaned.

"I guess I can't fool my Annie Bell," he laughed. Hannah glared at me and stood up suddenly. Her chair squeaked loudly across the floor. She threw her napkin on the table and then stalked out of the room.

I stared after her. What had I done this time? Dad pretended not to notice and just kept eating.

"This is sure delicious, Mary," he said, his voice soothing. He always was the peacemaker in our home.

"Thanks," Mom answered, but she wasn't smiling anymore. Her eyes flicked over to Hannah's empty chair from time to time.

After dinner I cleared the table and did the dishes, to Mom's surprise. I was hoping to convince her to let me use the car, thinking that working on the article for English with Corrie would be a good excuse. Mom came down as I was finishing up, and she had changed to a skirt. It came to me then what church thing I was supposed to go to. I groaned inwardly.

"You'd better get ready to go. We've got to leave in ten minutes. I'll wipe off the counters," she said. I knew there was no point in arguing. I was going to have to wait to see Mitch yet again. And I was going to be forced to see Sam. I gave in to the teenager in me and allowed the thought. *This totally stinks.*

Tuesday night was a huge deal for my family. Dad was the Scoutmaster, and Mom was in charge of Personal Progress for Young Women. Because Hannah, Dan, and I were all in the youth programs, we usually dropped Rachel off at Sister Jeppson's house and made a night of it. It was the one thing that as a teenager I'd never fought my parents on. I'd even volunteered to lead the music for our combined opening exercises. It might have had something to do with a certain handsome, brooding pianist.

When I was twelve, Sam and his mother and stepfather had moved to the neighborhood and started attending our church. Sister Sharp had been baptized a member as a child but hadn't really attended much or raised Sam that way. It wasn't till she met Brother Sharp, who claimed to be a devout Mormon, that she found religion again and dragged her son back to the fold. Fourteen-year-old Sam, who still went by his father's surname, hadn't wanted anything to do with church, but he was too scared of his stepfather to protest strongly.

I met Sam when I was staying late one Tuesday evening to help clean up, something that our family did frequently. As I walked through the deserted hall, gathering discarded handouts and crumpled napkins from the refreshments, I heard music coming from the chapel. Sam was there playing the piano as if he were drowning and the instrument was his life preserver. It was the most beautiful, painful thing I'd ever heard. I was fascinated by the thin, dark-eyed boy with all of his intensity, and I watched him closely for the next few months, looking for an opportunity to get to know him better.

When Bishop Michaels, looking for a way to reach the quiet boy, had asked Sam to play the piano for our Mutual opening exercises, I had immediately gone to him and volunteered my services as the chorister. It was a pathetic attempt. Even as a twelve-year-old I knew that. But I just had to be closer to Sam. Eventually Sam had started staying after meetings, too, to help our family clean up, and that was how I got to know more about his family and about what kind of man his stepfather, the so-called Christian, really was.

Now, as I changed into a denim skirt and dark blue tights, I decided that I might as well kill two birds with one stone. I tucked the manila envelope of music under my arm and determined that I'd talk to Sam about it that night.

It wasn't until we got to the church that it occurred to me that he might not show. He had never been there for any reason other than to keep the peace and make things easier for his mom. Would he decide not to come after the conversation we'd had earlier in the day? I scanned the parking lot, looking for his mother's car. I couldn't see it but knew that it could be on the other side of the building or they could just be running late. I decided to leave the envelope in the car so that I wouldn't look too eager with it. If he was there and he agreed to do the duet, then we could walk out to the car to get it. I tried not to wonder why I was putting so much mental effort into planning it all out.

Dan jogged off to sit with a bunch of other twelve-year-old boys, and my parents found a seat together. Hannah had bolted from the car the second we parked, and I hadn't seen her since. I took my usual place on the front row, forcing myself not to crane my head looking for Sam. I was actually feeling that same sense of anticipation I'd always felt on Tuesday nights, and it really bothered me. As the minutes ticked by and Sam didn't show, I prepared myself to take over on the piano. Sister Beader could always lead. Just as I was about to get up and walk to the piano, Sam swept past me, keeping his eyes carefully straight ahead, and took his seat. I took a deep breath, surprisingly feeling a little more relaxed now that he was here. It felt familiar and nostalgic.

Sam began to play.

The simple tune of "I Stand All Amazed" seemed more poignant and melodic when Sam played it. He had a gift for keeping things clean, nothing overly ornate or showy, yet he added a couple of extra chords and segues that made the music take on a deeper quality. I conducted the congregation, and we sang along, but my ears were mostly on the piano. Even though it was his second choice of instrument, he was amazing. Mr. Allan was right. Sam needed a music scholarship so that he could go to college and pursue his music career, not join the Air Force just because that was what his stepdad wanted him to do.

I loved music. It made me feel alive and happy. But Sam—he *was* music. Without music, he couldn't really be himself. I knew then that whether or not I wanted to avoid him, to prove how indifferent I was to him, I would do the duet in case it would help him to get a scholarship and be a musician for life. Maybe it was something I had always been meant to do.

I spent the rest of Young Women thinking about how to approach Sam with the music. I tried to think up clever things to say to make up for being so rude earlier. It seemed ironic that when I had finally found the ability to separate myself from him, telling him how I felt and how I didn't want to be around him anymore, that I was also able to start seeing him as a real person with his own needs and hurts and inadequacies. I had always seen him as the object of my affections. I was disturbed to realize just how prominently the word *object* appeared in that phrase. It made me ashamed of myself.

Sister Dupree was usually funny and entertaining, but tonight neither she nor the crafts could hold my attention for more than a minute at a time. Finally the activity came to an end, and the refreshments were served. I worked up the courage to go look for Sam. He was putting on his jacket and was just about to walk out of the door when I caught up with him.

"Sam, wait up."

He glanced up with a tight expression. He looked wary, but he waited.

I cleared my throat. "Hi. Sorry. Can we walk out to the car? I have something Mr. Allan wanted me to give to you."

He nodded shortly and held the door open for me, following me out into the cold night.

We walked to the parking lot without speaking, and I was trying to figure out the best way to apologize while still remaining firm in the boundaries that I was trying to establish. I opened the door and grabbed the envelope, removed the cello music, and handed it to him.

"What's this?" he asked, looking it over.

"It's a Schubert cello sonata. Mr. Allan wants us to play it in the Winterfest concert. He says he thinks it would be a great way to increase our chances for scholarships. I guess it would be a really good audition piece for you. He was hoping we could have at least had a run-through by Thursday."

Sam was scanning the music, and I could almost hear the notes issuing from his fingers as they absently fingered invisible strings.

"Hmmm. It's really beautiful. Schubert is a good choice, not as mainstream as Beethoven or Brahms. There is a fun little pizzicato section, too," he commented as he reviewed the music. Then he held it out to give back to me.

"What's the matter with it?" I asked.

"I'm not going to put you in an uncomfortable position. I can just do a solo or, you know, find another accompanist. It'll be fine," he said, trying to force the music into my hands.

"No, listen, Sam. I'm really sorry for going off on you like that earlier. I know it's not your fault that I've been all, I don't know—crazy, obsessed, or whatever. I've just been under a lot of strain these last couple of days, and you've been getting all the bad parts of that. I can't guarantee that I will be able to play this well enough to make it sound halfway decent, but I'm willing to try."

He still looked a little wary, but I pushed the music back toward him. "I'll even try to be civil, okay?"

"Annie, I'll do it, if you answer one question." Yikes, that left a much too large opening for me to stick my foot in my mouth again.

I hesitated. "How did I end up being the one to try to convince you to do this? It was Mr. Allan's idea, you know. Not mine." I didn't tell him I was just trying to help him out. I could only guess how well that would go over.

"How bad can one question be?" he asked, and there was a hint of that fire in his eyes again. I capitulated immediately.

"Fine. One question," I said, kicking myself the second the words left my lips. Those darn eyes.

"What changed?" He must have seen the confusion on my face because he hurried to clarify. "I mean between Sunday and Monday. What made you change your mind about me?" I rocked back to lean against the car. People were gradually drifting out to their cars, their refreshments consumed, and I knew it wouldn't be long before my family would be looking for me to help with cleanup. What could I say to Sam to explain the difference? I'd already spouted way too much in our previous conversations.

"Well, I'll tell you, but I want to ask you a question, too," I said. He nodded. "Okay. The thing that changed is that I'm in love with someone else."

"This Mitch person, right?"

"Yeah. You don't know him. He doesn't go to our school. He's a little . . . uh, older than we are," I said.

"He's older than I am?" he asked.

"Yes, but that's three questions now. It's my turn." He nodded. "My question for you is this. Why do you care? No, wait, I'm not trying to be rude. I just really want to understand. I mean, Sam, you have to look at this through my eyes. I think we've been friends, but it's never been anything more than that from you, no matter how much I wanted it to be more. It's been four years . . ." I stumbled over that number, knowing it had been much longer. "It's been four years, and this is the first time you've seemed to care if I was interested in someone else."

He stood quietly, and I grew more and more uncomfortable as I realized I was doing it again, focusing more on what I wanted—answers—than on what he needed. I didn't want to be that selfish person anymore.

"You know what, it doesn't matter. We can be friends, and we can play this duet, and it will be fun, right? We don't have to hash through all of this."

He studied my face for a minute and then nodded.

I went on. "You know, I think that if we are going to be friends, we are going to have to work on this communicating thing. I seem to always do the talking. I guess it's just another sign that we weren't meant to be together." I had meant it to sound light and joking, but it came across with more weight than I'd intended.

"I've always known that, Annie," he said quietly. He tucked the music under his arm and turned to walk away.

Chapter 13

I wanted to call out to stop him, but Mom showed up at that moment to call me back into the church. As I watched Sam walk away, part of me wanted him to explain what he meant by that cryptic comment, but the other part of me, the adult in me, realized that it didn't matter. It was better just to let it all go. I jogged back toward Mom and the church, then instantly regretted that decision as all my extra weight caught up with me and I ended up breathing too heavily for such a short distance.

"Man, I've really got to lose some weight," I gasped to Mom. "This is getting ridiculous."

Mom's laugh was a little startled as she ushered me inside.

"What were you two talking about?" she asked.

"I had to give him some music. Sam missed orchestra today, and Mr. Allan asked me to take it home for him." I could see the worry in Mom's eyes. "It's okay. Like I told you. I've moved on. It's just for school." I hurried back inside to finish helping with the cleanup. By the time everything was put away, Hannah had finally reappeared, and we loaded into the car.

"Where have you been, Hannah?" Dad asked as we pulled out of the church parking lot. "I didn't see you all night."

"I was talking to Sister Beader. I didn't feel like going to Young Women tonight," she said, keeping her face turned away from me.

"Why not?" Dad asked, but Mom waved her hand at him, and he dropped the subject. We picked up Rachel, and she and Dan immediately started fighting over a doughnut Dan had saved.

"It's mine. You had one already," Rachel whined.

"So what? It's mine." Dan tried to grab it out of her hands, and they tangled for a second, ramming into the back of Hannah's seat as we pulled into the driveway. She exploded.

"Knock it off, Dan. Do you have to always be an idiot? I can't stand it anymore! I hate living in this family!" She shoved the door open and stumbled out before the car even stopped moving. We could all hear her sobs as she ran toward the house and ducked under the still-rising garage door.

"Wow," Dan said. "What's the matter with her?"

"Dan, just lay off, please!" Mom said from the front seat. "I'll go talk to her. She's probably just having a bad day." But I could hear the exhaustion in her voice

"Mom, I think this is actually about Hannah and me. I'll try to talk to her first," I said.

Mom and Dad exchanged surprised looks. Mom opened her mouth like she was going to argue, but Dad shook his head at her.

"That's a good idea, baby cakes," he said. "Just remember that sometimes when someone is hurt they can't hear reason until they've licked their wounds."

"In other words, you should give her a little time to cool off," Mom said.

"I will," I said, climbing out of the car and going in the house to change.

Dad had nicknames for each of his children, besides the additions he made to our Christian names. I was "baby cakes." Rachel was "honey lamb." Dan was "sarge," and Hannah was "sugar plum." Her bedroom door had a sign on it that she had made at Activity Days—or maybe "Merrie Miss" is what we called it then. It was simple pink construction paper with a cutout from a magazine ad of the Sugar Plum Fairy from *The Nutcracker*, and it was adorned with the words "Sugar Plum's Domain." It was an old sign, something she'd made before the teenage angst settled in, and it was looking pretty worn. As I knocked on her door, I realized that Hannah had left that soft, feminine part of herself behind, and she had never reclaimed it since then. As an adult, Hannah was driven and career oriented. She had a live-in boyfriend, David, but she wasn't interested in marriage or having children or going to church. That left little common ground for us, and we really didn't have much of a relationship. In fact, we'd barely spoken in years other than exchanging cards on birthdays and for Christmas and seeing each other once or twice a year when she came home for Easter or Thanksgiving.

I knocked again, and she finally called out a very exasperated "Come in." I opened the door.

"Oh, it's you," she said. "Get out." She was lying on her stomach on her bed working on her homework. Her walls were completely plastered with posters of George Michael.

"I totally forgot about your George Michael thing," I said, walking in and closing the door behind me. She sat up and crossed her arms over her chest.

"Whatever, Annie. Just get out. I don't want to talk to you." She was trying really hard to sound angry, but I could hear the tears just under the surface.

"I know you don't want to talk to me. I get it. I'd like to talk to you, though," I said. She just glared at me. "Hannah, I know you're mad at me. I'm not sure of all the reasons, but I know that I've been selfish lately. I'm really trying hard to change, so I hope you can forgive me. If you want to blow up at me and yell, then it's okay. I can take it. Just yell at me. Tell me why you're mad. Get it off your chest." It felt like the right thing to do, noble even. Maybe if she yelled at me for a while, then she'd stop taking it out on the rest of the family.

"What? You think that just because Mom and Dad are all happy and joyful over the new you that I don't see what is really going on? What is the point of yelling at you? It's just one more reason to think that you are the center of the universe." Her voice had gone quiet. "You walk around here moping like you've lost everything in the world just because the guy you like doesn't like you back, and we are all supposed to just get out of the way and make things easy for you. Poor Annie, her life is so hard. Well, what about everyone else? Other people have lives, too, you know. Mom and Dad are constantly worrying about money, and now they have to spend it all on your therapy. You never help around the house. I do your chores half the time just so Mom doesn't have to do them. Now just because you made that stupid salad and cleaned your dump of a room, we are all supposed to forget what a total loser you've been? Well, I haven't forgotten, even if Mom and Dad have. You are still just as big a witch as always. I'm not even going to mention Travis."

"What? Travis who?" I latched onto that question, trying to ignore her other words, which were lodged somewhere under my ribcage.

"Travis Howard, Annie. The guy you are apparently asking to Girls' Choice, even though I told you I liked him. That Travis." Ah, the black-haired boy from the parking lot at school, I guessed.

"I didn't ask Travis to the dance. I haven't asked anyone, and I wasn't going to ask him anyway. Who even told you that?"

"Shawni overheard you and Corrie talking about it." Her voice was a little less bitter, and the tension in the room seemed to ease a bit. "You really aren't asking him?"

"No. I don't even want to go, but, well, I promised Corrie. I don't know who I'm going to ask." The conversation had taken a new turn, and I was relieved. Hannah's accusations had been far too close to the mark and not just about my teenage self.

"Look, Hannah, I know I've been a total slimeball. I can't make excuses for it, and I can't change the past, but I am trying to be a little better. I'm sorry for the garbage you've had to put up with, but maybe we can, you know, be friends or something? Hey, why don't you ask Travis to the dance and come with Corrie and me?"

Hannah didn't agree right away. Her sixteenth birthday had been only a couple of weeks ago. Would she be willing to do the asking for her very first date? Still, I could see her softening a little. "At least think about it?" I asked.

"I'll think about it," she said. It was a start. Suddenly things were awkward as we tried to find something else to talk about.

"So, George Michael, huh?" I finally asked.

"Yeah, what about him?" she said.

"Nothing. It's just, you know he's gay, right?"

Hannah rolled her eyes. "Whatever. You like your music, and I'll like mine."

"No, he's brilliant. I just mean he's, you know, into guys." I was regretting bringing this up.

"Ew, gross! No, he isn't. He just broke up with Brooke Shields," she said.

"Oh, my mistake," I said. This was just one more thing that had changed. Would I ever get used to it all? "I, uh, better get my homework done."

"Yeah, me, too," Hannah said. She turned her attention back to her books, and I closed the door quietly, smiling this time at the sign on her door.

Chapter
14

*B*ack in my room I thought over her words. I thought I was the center of the universe, that no one else had pain in their lives, and that I was the only thing that mattered? I moped around all the time? That completely summed up my life after Mitch's death. When was the last time I had thought about what anyone else was going through? I didn't really know what was happening in the lives of my siblings and parents unless it specifically intruded upon my life. My neighbors were all like props for me to react against. I didn't remember anyone else experiencing joy or tragedy around me. It was all about me.

And my children. I clung to that thought as a reassurance that I wasn't the most selfish person on the planet. I cared about my kids, and I tried to make them happy. Even as I thought about it, though, I realized that I only vaguely cared about their schooling as long as they were generally doing well. All I really cared about was that they seemed happy. Now I asked myself if they were just props in my life, too. Did I love them because they were inherently valuable little people or because they filled a need of mine?

I fell asleep with those disturbing questions running through my mind, looking for answers that I didn't have.

The next morning brought a renewed sense of purpose and determination with it. I still didn't know the answers to the questions I had asked myself the night before, but in my sleep, it seemed, I had formed a new resolution that burst upon me the moment I woke. Whatever my past behavior had been, both my past as a teenager and my past as a wife and mother, my future didn't have to be the same way. I could start today to try to be less selfish, to really see other people and the pain that they might be living with, and maybe I could even do something about it.

It was the same realization I had had about Sam the evening before, but now it was clear that it was a much wider problem than I had known.

With that goal in mind, I tried to focus on other people as I moved through my day. At breakfast I asked Rachel and Dan about school and their friends. On the way to school I discovered that Mom was planning on grocery shopping that afternoon, her least favorite chore, and offered to do it for her. She accepted with a little bit of skepticism and a smile. I got to school feeling pretty good about the start of my day. I could do this. It felt really good, actually.

When I got to World History, Corrie was waiting outside the classroom for me with a determined look on her face.

"Annie, it's Wednesday. I'm starting to freak out. Most of the guys I know have already been asked, and now Angela just told me that Hannah is asking Travis, so there goes that idea. Seriously, why would she do that? She is such a brat!"

"Corrie, I told Hannah to ask Travis. She really likes him, and I didn't want to go out with him anyway. I told her that they should come with us to the dance." Corrie's mouth dropped open.

"You invited her to come with us?" she repeated loudly, as if testing my hearing. Or maybe my intelligence. "I thought you hated her." She was shaking her head in disbelief, her poodle hair bouncing around her shoulders.

"I don't hate her. She's my sister. We just bug each other a lot of the time, but we had this great talk last night, and she was telling me . . ."

"Okay, whatever. You still have to figure out what you are going to do. Who are you going to ask now? I mean, I'm racking my brain here, but unless you want to go with a total loser, you are basically down to two options. And you're not going to like either one."

"Okay, what are they?" I asked, figuring I would just get through this and make it happen. It was so important to Corrie. I wouldn't let her down.

"Your options are Sam. Or Sam." She smiled weakly at her joke. I didn't smile in return. "Look, I told you that you wouldn't like the choices. Annie, please. Please do this for me. He isn't going with anyone yet. Angela talked to Andrew, and he told her that Miranda asked Sam but Sam said no. I think he just wants you to ask him."

I fought down the interest that surged through me at that juicy bit of gossip. I thought about our conversation last night in the church parking lot. Maybe I could ask him, and he would get that it was just a friends thing. Maybe. Still, the thought of it made my stomach wrap up in a huge knot.

"I'll think about it," I finally said. The halls were emptying, and the first bell rang. "Let's go inside. It's time for class."

"Fine, but you can't think about it for too long. You have to ask someone *today*. Seriously, the dance is in two days. You can't keep putting it off, okay?" I nodded again. The knot grew.

Mr. Croft moved into the hall and started shooing people into class. We took our seats as the second bell rang.

One thing that was great about Mr. Croft was that he didn't actually expect anyone to listen to him. As long as it was relatively quiet, meaning he could hear himself think, then he would continue the lecture and expect that we would all take notes. Note taking wasn't common, however, so many kids relied heavily on someone copying the answers for the test, usually left casually on his desk, and then distributing them to everyone else.

When I had been sixteen—the first time—I had copied those answers without any feelings of guilt, just worrying about getting caught. Now as the list was passed surreptitiously under desks, finally making its way to me, I felt guilty for a moment. It wasn't guilt for me. I'd already graduated, after all. But it was guilt that I was letting it go when all of these children around me were missing out on the opportunity to actually learn something. I held the folded piece of paper for a minute or two, debating. Then I forced myself to pay attention to Mr. Croft, whose monotone voice and dry recitation created a haze of confusion and sleepiness that drifted over the class like heavy smog. *Forget it,* I thought. *No one could be expected to listen to that.* I quickly copied down the answers and passed the paper to Corrie, sitting behind me.

With my mind freed from the obligation of paying attention to the lecture, the tasks I had ahead of me loomed large in my mind. In order to be there for Corrie, I had to ask someone to the dance. According to her, the only source of information I had on the subject, the only person left to ask was Sam. Now the question I had to ask myself was, Could I do it? Could I ask him to a dance knowing that it would give the wrong impression? Could I ask him to the dance knowing that Mitch was alive? Wouldn't that be cheating?

Wait! A new thought came to me, something that I felt ridiculous for not having considered before. I wanted to slap myself in the head for being such a fool. I hurriedly twisted around in my seat. Corrie was resting her head in one hand and doodling in her notebook. The names "Jesse" and "Corrie Marie Lingstrom" were scrawled a dozen times in different colors of ink and stylized letters. I shoved away an image of Corrie as Mrs. Jerk-face Lingstrom and hurried to ask her my question.

"Corrie, can I borrow your car during lunch? I need to do something really important." I stopped whispering, not knowing how to explain it. She took in my excited expression and started to smile.

"Is this about the dance?" she stage-whispered. "Did you come up with an idea of how to ask him? Maybe you could get like ten of those 100 Grand candy bars and tape them to his door and say something like 'It would be worth more than a million dollars to me if you'd go to Girls' Choice.' No, don't do that. It's lame."

"Thanks for the idea, though," I murmured, trying not to laugh. "That's not exactly what I was thinking of, but this is about the dance. You might need to help me get out of Music Theory early, though. I don't know if I'll have time otherwise."

"No problem. I have the perfect idea. You just have to hint that it's, you know, a *girl* problem. Mr. Allan gets totally freaked out by that kind of stuff. I'll handle it," she said. I smiled as she whispered more suggestions about "cute" ways that I could ask Sam to the dance. I wasn't ready to disabuse her of the idea. The knot in my stomach from earlier was gone now, replaced instead by butterflies of anticipation.

Now that I had a plan in place, the clock seemed to slow down until each click of the second hand was a distinct, deliberate event. I found myself checking the time every two or three minutes and thinking that at least ten had passed. Finally, though, the bell rang, and I wasn't the only one to burst out of the classroom with a heartfelt sigh of relief. Corrie was full of excitement and ideas, and I let her babble on, her mood, if not her words, echoing my own.

I was a distracted mess in Music Theory, resuming my clock-watching and waiting for the halfway point so that I could make a break for it. Corrie's keys were tucked safely in my pocket, my ticket to freedom. Sam's back on the front row couldn't even distract me, not really. I had looked at him once when he first entered the room. But he'd stared straight ahead, not even sending so much as a blink in my direction. Apparently our conversation hadn't really smoothed things over as well as I had hoped. After that I ignored him and just focused on what I was about to do.

The forty minutes passed slowly, but finally Corrie nudged me, and I nodded. I made a bit of a show of leaning over and whispering in her ear, then made a hurried exit from the room. Behind me I knew she would go to the front of the class and whisper something to Mr. Allan, who would look a little pale and wave her back to her seat, and my excuse would be made. I made a beeline for the restroom and waited for five minutes. I took the opportunity to brush through my hair and put on a little bit of lip gloss, wishing that I had taken a little longer in getting ready this morning. When I figured enough time had passed, I poked my head out of the door to scan the hall. The coast was clear.

I hurried to the side door and reached out to push it open when a voice stopped me.

"Leaving school grounds?" Sam asked.

I groaned, spinning around. He was leaning casually against the wall. "What are you doing here?" I asked.

"Are you going to see that guy?" he asked, shoving himself away from the wall and walking toward me.

A little thrill went up my spine at his approach, but I pushed it back down quickly.

"No, I'm not feeling well. I'm going home," I lied.

"Really? Then why didn't you tell that to Mr. Allan?"

"Um, excuse me, but what business is it of yours?" I was starting to get annoyed. I really needed to get out of here. It had taken me too long to get to this point, and I wasn't going to let anything stand in my way now. I turned my back on Sam and pushed through the door. The sky was dark with gathering storm clouds, and the temperature had dropped abruptly. I wrapped my arms around myself as I walked quickly to the parking lot, scanning it for Corrie's car.

"This is really a bad idea, you know." Sam's voice close behind made me jump. I thought he'd stayed behind in the school. I ignored him and kept walking. I spotted her car at the end of the far row, trying to focus on my mission and not on the following footsteps. I tried to unlock the door, but the key wouldn't turn. I tried it again. It slid in smoothly but wouldn't turn.

"If he is older than I am, then he's too old for you, and if you're sneaking off to see him in the middle of school, that means that your parents don't know or don't approve. Not smart, Annie."

"So, what, you're my protector now? Very funny. It's not your business, Sam, as I believe I mentioned already. Please go back to class and leave me alone." I tried the key again, still without success.

"Is it even legal for him to date you? I mean, how old is he? Nineteen? Twenty? Do you want him to go to jail?" Sam asked with that same half-sarcastic voice he'd been using the whole time. I tried the key one more time, anger flaring up when it wouldn't work again.

"So help me, Sam!" I yelled and turned, ready to throw the keys at him. He ducked and held up his hands.

"Hey, hey, calm down." He reached out and plucked the keys from my fingers.

Mitch's brother Charlie had always liked to tease us about our age difference. Finally, out of sheer annoyance I had looked it up so that I could prove how wrong he was.

"For your information, he's twenty-three and no, it's not illegal to date me, although technically it's not illegal to date anyone of any age. It's just illegal to have sex. And we aren't having sex since we haven't even met yet. Even if we were, it still wouldn't be illegal since he's not more than ten years older than I am. Now give me those keys and go. Away. Now!" I practically yelled the last three words and tried to grab the keys from him, but he dangled them just out of my reach.

"You lost me again, but I got that you aren't dating him and that you seem to know way too much about that law."

I took another swipe at getting the keys, but he dodged around me and deftly unlocked the passenger door. "Get in."

"How did you do that?" I asked.

"Easy. I just used the right key. Get in, and I'll drive," he said, gesturing to the seat.

"Uh-uh," I said. "There is no way that is going to happen."

"Okay. Fine with me," he said and promptly pocketed the keys.

"Sam! I need to go now! You are wasting my time!" I felt like crying, something that was becoming far too frequent for my taste.

"Look, you have two choices. Either you let me drive you to wherever it is or I go back inside and tell Mr. Allan that you are cutting class. It's your choice."

I stared at him, open-mouthed, trying to decide what I should do. Even if I could get those keys out of his pocket, would he actually rat me out to Mr. Allan? Would Mr. Allan believe Sam over me? I already knew the answer to that. Mr. Allan worshipped the musical ground Sam walked on. I realized once again that one of the curses of being an adult in a teenager's life is that I had a much more complete under-standing of the consequences of my actions. My teenage self wouldn't have cared about the consequences of cutting class. Now, I could see all too clearly just what kinds of trouble I would be dealing with at home and how difficult that would make things for me and for my family. What was I thinking? My teenage self would never have been in this bizarre situation in the first place.

I sighed in defeat.

"Fine, you drive, but you will stay in the car, and you will keep your opinions to yourself," I said. He studied my face for a second, tak-ing in my glare with a smile.

"Deal. Get in." He gestured once more to the passenger seat with a flourish, and I ungraciously flopped onto the seat just as the rain started to come down.

Trying to ignore him as he drove, I stared straight ahead and spoke only when giving him directions. Sam turned on the radio and scanned through the stations until he found a song he liked, something with a wailing guitar by Whitesnake, I thought. Then he turned it up and leaned back against the seat and sang along, completely undis-turbed by my stony silence and tightly folded arms. I tried to stay mad. I thought about all of the inconveniences that Sam had created in my life, especially in the last three days. He had really tried to mess with my head. But I was finally on my way. Right now, I was finally headed to Mitch's house, and in just a few minutes I would be able to see him breathing, young, healthy. Alive. I couldn't help the smile that spread across my face.

"Am I forgiven?" Sam asked, noticing my smile.

"Hardly. Still, you can't ruin my mood today. I'm too happy for you to mess it up," I said. "Turn left at the next light." We drove for a few more minutes in silence. As we got closer to Mitch's neighborhood, my heart started to speed up.

"Are you sure you're not sick? You look a little flushed to me," Sam said. I just rolled my eyes.

"Take a right here, then the first left."

We turned, and we were in Mitch's neighborhood. The road was carpeted by freshly fallen leaves, and stately old homes stood on either side of the road.

"Seriously, Annie. Maybe I should take you home after all," Sam said. I looked at him in alarm, but he was grinning. "Don't freak out. I'm just teasing you. I wouldn't miss this for the world."

"What is that supposed to mean?" I said, smacking him on the arm. "Whoa, watch out!" He glanced back at the road just in time to avoid hitting a blue truck that was headed in the other direction. "If you weren't going to pay attention, then you should have let me drive. There, that brick house with the pine tree. That's it. Pull over here."

Sam parked the car across the street, and I stared out the window through the rain at Mitch's mother's house. My stomach was doing somersaults, and my heart was racing.

This was it.

Chapter
15

Mitch's dad had passed away when Mitch was only eleven, and Margaret had raised Mitch and his younger brother, Charlie, all on her own. She never remarried, said she didn't need to when she already had two of the most handsome men on the earth. She had been a wonderful mother-in-law, not the crazy, controlling type that I'd always heard stories about. My relationship with my own mother was always strained, and in Margaret I found a listening ear, a comforting touch, and a refusal to judge. She was the reason that Mitch was such an amazing husband and father.

When Mallory was four and I was expecting Jenna, Margaret decided to shovel her walks. Charlie was living out of state, and it seemed she didn't want to take Mitch away from his family to come and take care of her, so she put on her boots and her gloves and crunched out into the snow. We got the call at eight the next morning. She'd collapsed in her driveway and wasn't found until Mr. Caspar, the neighbor across the street, left for work the next morning. It had been a fairly mild heart attack, and she probably would not have died had it not been for the cold and the length of time she'd lain there.

Mitch was devastated. We both were, but he felt it was his fault. For the rest of his life he carried the burden of guilt for not shoveling her walks that morning so she wouldn't have tried to do it herself.

Now, as I sat here in Corrie's car with Sam in the driver's seat staring at me, I could see Margaret's silhouette behind the curtains as she moved about the living room. The lights were on inside against the gloom of the rainy morning, and Margaret moved from one end of the room to the other. It looked like she might be dusting.

"Are you going to go to the door?" Sam asked after about five minutes.

I nodded, but my hand didn't reach for the door handle. Now that I was there I wondered what on earth I was possibly going to say. All of my attention had been focused on getting here. What now? Did I think I could really waltz up to his door and ask him to the dance?

"Do you want me to go with you?" Sam asked.

That got my attention. I turned to look at him, suddenly registering the fact that it was Sam who was sitting here with me.

"Sam, what on earth are you doing here? Why did you want to come, anyway?" I asked.

"You first," he said.

"What do you mean?"

"You first. Why did you come here?" he prodded. "To sit in the car and stare at that house? What's your plan?"

"I wish I knew," I sighed, hopefully too quietly for him to hear me, then I grasped the door handle and made a dash for it before I could think too long and talk myself out of it. The rain was really coming down, and I was drenched by the time I got to the cover of the front porch. I wondered if it was possible for a sixteen-year-old to have a heart attack. My chest felt too tight to breathe, but I raised my hand and rang the bell.

"One minute," I heard Margaret's muffled voice from inside and then footsteps. The door opened, and she was there. Her blue eyes, just like Mitch's, were wrinkled at the corners with her smile, and she was so real, so alive, it took my breath away. Tears sprang to my eyes as it all came rushing in at me. I realized that she was speaking, and I suddenly snapped back to focus.

"I'm so sorry, what was that?" I asked.

"What can I do for you, dear?" she repeated in her kind voice. There was that hint of an Irish accent that I had so loved from our first meeting.

"Yes, um. Is Mitch here?" I asked, recalling my purpose for

coming. I wanted to stare at her for hours, but I was here for something even more important. Someone even more precious to me.

"I'm sorry. He just left with his brother. They should be home later this evening. Is there something I can help you with, dear?" I could see the curiosity in her face, and I wondered what she must be thinking about a teenage girl looking for her twenty-three-year-old son. I saw it all, but disappointment was ripping through me with such power it threatened to buckle my legs underneath me. I took a long, slow breath in, telling myself that I would just have to try again. Margaret must have seen something in my look because she threw me a lifeline.

"Would you like to leave a message for him?" she asked. I nodded in relief.

"Yes, that would be perfect," I said.

She excused herself to get a pen and paper. I glanced inside with longing, missing the elegant and old-fashioned living room with her collections of thimbles and spoons displayed in cases along the wall. The smell of her freshly baked cinnamon rolls poured out of the front door. Of course, with Mitch home after another year of absence, Margaret would be baking up a storm in celebration, the way she celebrated everything.

She returned and handed me a pen and notepad. I thought briefly about writing an explanation of who I was but immediately thought better of it. Instead I simply scrawled my parents' phone number, my name, and the words "Please call tonight. It's very important." I folded the paper and wrote Mitch's name on the front, and then handed everything back to Margaret. She took the items and placed them on the entryway table before turning back to me.

"I'll make sure Mitch gets the note as soon as he and Charlie return."

She waited for me to say something, but I just nodded. I knew I needed to walk away now, but I couldn't turn my back on her yet. Without a word, I leaned forward and gave her a quick hug, breathing in her lavender scent. She slowly raised her arms and patted my back. To my horror, those stupid teenage emotions hit again, and a sob welled up and bubbled over. Margaret's arms tightened around me, and she smoothed my hair. She was so familiar and comforting, and I couldn't help myself. I clung to her for another long moment, allowing myself to share my pain with the one woman in the world who could possibly understand it. I knew she didn't right now, but somewhere in the future, in heaven or whatever afterlife there was, Margaret would be the one who could really understand. She had lost her husband while her children were young, and she loved Mitch just as much as I did. I knew that much, and I shared it with her, then I forced myself to pull away and smile in embarrassment.

"I'm so sorry, Mar . . . I mean Mrs. Kelly. I don't know what got into me." I wiped at my face. Margaret was studying me.

"It's no problem, dear. Being young is hard sometimes," she said. I smiled.

"You can say that again," I said, sniffing. "Please make sure Mitch gets that?" She nodded, and I waved and ran back toward the car. The rain was turning positively torrential, and I ducked inside the car gratefully. Sam was waiting for me. I had forgotten about him.

"Not there?" he asked.

"Nope. He left with Charlie just a few . . . wait! That blue truck!" I shouted.

"What blue truck?" Sam asked in surprise.

"The one you almost hit. That's Charlie's truck. I totally forgot about that thing. I think he got rid of it right after . . . never mind. I missed him." My throat constricted as tears bubbled up behind my eyes.

"He was right there, and I didn't see him because you were distracting me. If you had just left me alone, I would have gotten here in time, and I wouldn't be sitting here with you." My voice broke. I had been so close. "If it weren't for you, I would be with him. RIGHT! NOW!" I yelled and cried at the same time. It was too much. All of the pain and the anticipation and the frustration came pouring out of me, and I collapsed in tears that left me unable to speak.

Chapter

16

*S*am silently started the car and drove back to the school. I cried all the way. I knew I could try again, but it just seemed so cruel that I had been that close, had seen the truck but hadn't looked up. I had missed Mitch by seconds. Eventually, though, the tears began to dry. I had started to theorize that maybe as a teenager I had a certain number of tears allotted for each day. Maybe today I had reached my quota, and when they were gone I could calm down and think clearly. As the sobs quieted into sniffles and finally into a long drawn-out sigh, Sam finally ventured to speak.

"Annie, I'm sorry for whatever I did that messed things up," he said. I looked over and saw a pained look cross his face. "I just kind of feel like . . . I don't know. It's like I have to make sure that you're—okay, I guess."

"You feel like it's your job to make sure I'm okay?" I asked. He nodded slowly. "Wow, that's really horrible."

"What? Why?"

"Because even though I've tried apologizing and telling you that it's not your fault and all of that stuff, I still managed to make you feel like you are somehow responsible for my teenage drama. It's depressing. Look, Sam, I mean it when I say that I'm fine," I said.

He raised his eyebrows in disbelief. "Really, Annie? You're fine? Because from where I sit it seems like you've been a complete mess for the past three days. You've been ripping my head off, getting in fights with your sister . . ."

My mouth dropped open. How did he know about that? He leaned closer, his voice softer, more husky. "And every time I see you, it seems you've just been crying or are just about to start crying. So how is that supposed to qualify as okay? I don't get it. It's like in the last three days you've completely gone off the deep end."

"So delivering a bogus suicide note to your house was not being off the deep end? This is worse than that?" I shot back. I was *not* going to be distracted by his nearness.

"I knew the note wasn't real. I'm not blind. I can see that you tend to be a little, you know, dramatic. This, though, this whole thing with some old guy—*that's* scary to me." He slapped the signal a little too hard, and the windshield wipers kicked up to a frantic pace until he readjusted them.

"If you knew I wasn't serious, then why did you tell me that it freaked you out?" I almost yelled. I'd been beating myself up for that stupid mistake for years, only to find out he'd known it was a fake all along? How *dare* he be angry with *me?*

"Because it forced me to realize what was going on. I wasn't sure how I felt about the fact that you were interested in me. It was easier when we could just be friends." He blew out a frustrated breath. "Yeah, it was *so much* easier."

That sucked away all my anger and frustration and left me deflated.

"I know. I told you it was stupid," I said quietly, and I couldn't keep the bitterness out of my voice. "I keep telling you, though. You don't have to worry about my being in love with you anymore."

Sam pulled the car into the parking lot and slammed it into park.

He was staring straight ahead with a grim expression. There was a muscle in his jaw that stood out slightly as he clenched his teeth. "What if I'm not okay with that?" he asked, his voice barely above a whisper. My eyes shot to his face.

"Sam, what does that even mean?" I almost pleaded. "I'm just so confused."

"You think *you* are confused," he laughed, a short sound without any real humor in it. "This is all I know: You have been there when no one else noticed I was alive. At first you were just a little girl, you know. And I thought it was sweet that you wanted to hang around me, but that was it. I mean, I was fourteen and an idiot, okay? Whenever my stepdad was being a—well, you seemed to understand and care about me, and I appreciated it. Probably more than you can ever know. But you had your perfect family. You have no idea what it's really like to live in my house. I couldn't tell you about how bad it really was, sometimes still is. No, I couldn't tell you the whole story, but I craved talking to you. I have always loved that. You have such a crazy, interesting way of seeing things," he said. He took a deep breath and turned to look at me, and a jolt ran through me, that electric feeling that was so familiar around him. His eyes locked onto mine, and I couldn't break that contact.

"I never knew, though, Annie. I had no idea that you were interested in me as anything more than a friend. I mean, how could you be? When you left that note at my house, it did scare me at first, but only for a few seconds. I called your mom because I knew I needed to, just in case, but then I went after you to try to catch up and tell you . . ." He paused.

"Tell me what?" I asked breathlessly. The sixteen-year-old in me hoped desperately for a very specific answer.

"Tell you that you shouldn't love me," he said.

Disappointment flooded me. How stupid that he still had the power to disappoint me like that.

"Oh, well, then I guess you should be relieved . . ."

"Wait! I'm not finished," he said. "Just hear me out and stop jumping to conclusions, okay?"

I nodded, and he took a deep breath, holding it for a second and then letting it out in a whoosh. "You said that you are going to marry this Mitch guy. Well, I know we're still young, but that's exactly what I see in your future. You are the kind of girl who gets married and has four or five kids and drives carpool and cooks roast beef on Sundays, just like all the other church ladies. You don't see what life for me is like. I don't know how to fit into a life like that." There was a long silence as I digested this new perspective on Sam's opinion of me.

"You're right," I said, finally. "That is who I am meant to be. I am going to get married and have three kids, two girls and a boy, and I'm going to be very happy."

There was silence again. He was right. I was going to do all of those things, and it was going to bring me joy. So much joy that when it was time for it to come to an end, I would no longer know how to go on living. In that moment my longing for my children was nearly suffocating. Underneath it, though, there was pain in the piece of my heart that had always belonged solely to Sam. Something he had said wriggled up to the surface of my thoughts.

"You are telling me that you can't be part of my life because it's not who you are, right?" He nodded. "Then why did you say that you weren't okay with my not being interested in you anymore?"

He gave me a sad smile but didn't speak for a long moment. He seemed to be warring within himself. He opened his mouth to speak and then closed it again as he turned to stare out the window. When he spoke, he didn't turn, and his voice was quiet. I had to strain to hear him.

"I don't know how to do it, to be part of your life, but I can't stand the thought of you with someone else, either. You talk about him like you already know exactly what's ahead in your future, how many kids you're going to have, when it's going to happen, all of that kind of stuff, then you turn around and say you haven't even met him yet. I don't know what's going on with that, but I do know this. I've tried hard to not think about my future. It doesn't look that great, you know. My mom and Leonard don't have any money, my grades are no good, I don't know if I'll get to go to college, but I want to get out of that house as soon as possible. That's about as far as my future planning has gone." His voice dropped down to nearly a whisper. "Still, whenever I do think about my future, I can't picture it without you in it. You would be totally fine without me, but I wouldn't make it through a day without you." He didn't look back but placed the keys on the dashboard, opened the door, and dashed into the rain.

Those stupid teenage emotions. I guess my quota for tears hadn't been reached for the day, after all.

Chapter

17

I don't want to talk about it," I said for the tenth time in the last five minutes.

"Why not? How bad could it really have been? Did he tell you to drop dead or call you names or something?" Corrie asked again, refusing to let the subject drop. She dropped her bag in the backseat of her car and climbed inside.

"No, he didn't say anything about the dance," I said. *That's because we didn't talk about the dance at all,* I thought. *No, just about how he actually really did want me in his life, and now I know I was wrong for all of those years, and most of the pain I went through as a teenager was completely unnecessary.*

"Well, what did he say, then, that has had you so mopey all day? Really? What could be so bad?" she asked.

"I don't want to talk about it, Corrie. Just drop it, okay?" I snapped. She started the engine but didn't pull out.

"Annie, what is the matter with you?" she asked angrily. "Something is different this week, and I've been trying my best to, like, be your best friend and be all supportive and all that. It's just not working, though. I don't know what you want, okay? You used to tell me everything, and you used to care about what was going on in my life, too. You haven't asked me about Jesse once this week, other than ripping on him for no reason."

"That's because I know you can do so much better than him, Corrie."

"Butt out! Why do you say stuff like that when it's clear that you don't even care what my life is like? It's just all about you. Well, I'm sick of it, okay? I have my own problems and my own stuff to deal with. You don't seem to think that the dance is that big of a deal, but I really do, okay? It's a big deal to me." She sat with her arms folded and glared out the window.

I wanted to reach out and comfort her, but I was too exhausted to move. Besides, everything she said was too close to the truth. The silence stretched on, broken only by the sound of the rain on the windshield and the low rumble of the engine.

"Look," she continued more quietly. "I talked to Angela today. She is going with Andrew, and she invited me and Jesse to double with them. So, you don't have to act like you care about it anymore. I've got it covered."

I knew I should apologize, but all I could feel was relief. Corrie wouldn't be alone with Jesse, and I didn't have to figure out who to ask and go through all that awkwardness. Still, I'd never wanted to hurt her.

"I'm really sorry, Corrie," I said, opening the door. "It's probably best for me to walk home today."

She just shrugged, and I stepped out into the rain, closing the door behind me. She pulled out immediately, tires squealing on the wet pavement, and drove away.

As I trudged home in the freezing rain, I thought about Corrie and Sam and Hannah—and all of the other people I had hurt. When I first woke up in my bedroom, back in this body and this time, it had seemed to be a dream. As time went on and I realized that I was actually here, it had seemed logical that there was something that I needed to do, a wrong to right or someone to help. Instead, I just hurt everyone more. Maybe I was here as punishment for being such a failure as a mom.

My children's faces danced in front of my eyes, and the tears came again. These weren't teenage emotions. My heart was breaking that I was living in a world where my children didn't exist. The way that things were going, so differently from how I remembered them, filled me with fear that they never would exist, either. What if I never could meet up with Mitch? What if that all changed? It felt like the universe or God or whatever was controlling my life was keeping us separated and pushing me together with Sam. What would that mean for my future? For Mallory and Jenna and James?

The rain poured down, mixing with my tears as I walked slowly, unable to force myself to hurry despite the cold. By the time I walked in the door I was shivering violently. The house was, thankfully, empty with everyone else at school or work or errands. I climbed the stairs and went to my room, dropping my bag inside the door and collapsing on my bed. Vaguely the thought came that I should change out of my wet clothes, but it seemed a distant and unimportant idea, obscured by the fog of grief that surrounded me. I just curled into a ball and cried, ignoring the shivers that racked my body. At some point I lost track of why I was even crying. Perhaps it was because I missed Mitch so much, or maybe it was my longing for our children. Maybe it was disappointment in the mess I seemed to make of everything or the tortured look on Sam's face as he got out of the car. Whatever the reason, probably all of them combined, I cried until I fell asleep.

Chapter

18

I knew I was dreaming because Mitch was there. He stood in a grassy meadow, looking very tall and handsome in his tuxedo. Rows of chairs stood on either side of an aisle lined with flowers. The tall grass brushed against my long train as I walked toward him. I blushed as I caught his expression. He was looking at me with an intense appreciation. I glanced around, relieved to see that we were alone. He was so good-looking and his blue eyes were filled with so much love it almost hurt to look at him.

I walked slowly, each step deliberate as I moved toward him and watched his smile gradually grow. After about five steps or so, I realized he wasn't getting any closer. He smiled and held out his hands to me, and I picked up the pace of my steps, hurrying now. But no matter how quickly I walked, he stayed just as far away. I passed row after row, all beribboned and bedecked with flowers, and suddenly I could hear my shoes clicking as the grass turned to wooden floor.

And Mitch was still just as many steps away.

His smile faltered, and there was an expression of disappointment on his face. I could read the thought in his eyes, *Why aren't you coming to take my hand?* I tried to tell him I was coming, but I couldn't force the words out. I ran faster, but now he wasn't staying in one place, and he began to drift away. Shadowy walls sprang up around me, creating a room that expanded in length until I was looking at Mitch at the end of a long tunnel. I moved to pick up the train of my wedding dress and sprint even faster, but my hands encountered only a knee-length skirt. I realized in horror that I was wearing the black dress I had purchased for Mitch's funeral. My ears started to ring, and I screamed as the tunnel grew so long that Mitch was no longer in sight. I stood alone in a chapel with only a casket, black and cold, looming in front of me.

The ringing in my ears intensified until it was shrill and piercing and, with a start, I sat up in bed to the sound of the telephone. I was disoriented, unsure of how long I had been sleeping. I stumbled down the hall to my parents' room, trying to reach the phone, but my mother was already there. She picked up the receiver.

"Hello? Who? No, I'm sorry, there's no one here by that name. No, it's no problem. Good-bye." She hung up the phone and then looked up with a start. "Annie. You scared me. I didn't know you were home."

She took a long look at me, and her eyes grew wide. I felt another shiver rip through me, banging my teeth together violently. "Honey? Are you sick?" She hurried over to me and felt my forehead with the back of her hand. "You're soaked. Why didn't you change your clothes? Annie? Honey?" I heard her speaking but I couldn't answer, my teeth were chattering so hard. Her voice grew in volume and pitch. "Annie? Come on. Let's get you in the tub." She ushered me into the bathroom and filled the tub with hot water while she stripped me down and wrapped me in a thick towel. I let her do it, not having the energy to protest.

The water was almost too hot against my icy skin, and I eased in bit by bit, allowing each part of my body to acclimate to the temperature.

The hot water began to work its magic, and the tension gradually leached out of my muscles. Mom made sure I was warming up before she left to get me some hot peppermint tea. I sank down into the water, letting it cover my ears as if I could block out the noises in my head. As the cold gradually seeped away, I was left with an overwhelming sense of confusion and fear. It had suddenly hit me on the way home just how trapped I was, how any choice I made had the potential for colossal disaster. I had come within seconds of seeing Mitch. I still ached for it more than anything. But the fight with Corrie and the revelation with Sam had made me realize now just how dangerous that could have been.

What would I have done, anyway? Ask a twenty-three-year-old stranger to my high school dance? I shuddered, knowing that was exactly what I would have done.

Mom came back in with the tea, and I sipped the hot, fragrant liquid gratefully, allowing it to warm me inside while the water continued to warm my skin. The questions kept bubbling up through the steamy haze.

So what if I *had* asked him to the dance? Would it have messed everything up? Would it have meant that we embarked on a course that diverged from the one I had followed originally? What if it meant I would never have had my life with him? Would my children never even have been born? That fear had nagged at me before but somehow hadn't really hit me until today. I had no idea what to do now. Anything I did could take me in a direction that I didn't want to go. How could I live through this life again without changing anything? I didn't remember enough of my life to be able to duplicate it exactly. I wasn't the same person now that I had been as a teenager. It seemed inevitable that if I stayed here I would ruin everything. That left me with just one question.

The water was starting to cool, and the shivers were returning. I drained the tub enough to make room for more hot water, all the while considering that question.

How could I get back to my life? It was a hard life in many ways, but I knew now that I wouldn't trade it. I had spent thirteen years with the most amazing man in the world, someone who loved me unconditionally and made me truly happy. I had three beautiful, intelligent, funny children who meant everything to me. I needed to get home to them. It stood to reason that if I had somehow traveled back in time, then there had to be a way to get home again. What was it?

That was the question that I latched on to. What could I do to get home again? My thoughts spun in circles as I looked for an answer. I even considered whether there was anyone I could talk to about it. I couldn't think of a single person who would take me seriously and be able to help me. I was, by all empirical evidence, an overly dramatic sixteen-year-old who had recently threatened to commit suicide and was now in the care of a psychologist. Who was going to believe that I was really a thirty-eight-year-old, time-traveling mother of three? I laughed out loud at the thought, my sarcastic mirth turning suddenly into a deep cough.

The water had cooled again, so I drained the tub and wrapped up in a towel, then went to my room. My limbs felt like Jell-O with all my strength gone. I shivered while I found some comfortable sweats and a T-shirt and dug in my drawer for my thickest socks. I added two extra blankets to my bed and climbed in, my hair still wrapped in a towel, and tried to force my brain to come up with a solution to this impossible situation.

I heard the garage door open and Mom left, probably to pick up Dan and Rachel. I remembered now that I had promised to do the grocery shopping. Just the thought of leaving my room, even leaving my bed, was too frightening. I stayed huddled under the quilts, playing over and over in my head every mistake I had made in the past few days. The list was long, and I shuddered to think how many there were that I didn't even know about. I heard Mom return with the kids, but then my attention faded back to my fear again. The hours passed as I drifted back and forth between those frantic, searching thoughts and the reality of my surroundings. The next thing I knew, it was dark and Mom was calling everyone to dinner.

Hannah knocked and then opened the door a crack.

"Mom wants to know if you are coming down for dinner," she asked. I tried to force myself to pay attention to her words, and it occurred to me, somewhere in the back of my mind, that her tone was civil. Concerned even.

"No, thanks," I said, hoarsely. "I don't feel up to it."

Hannah shrugged and was about to close the door when I remembered something.

"Hey, Hannah, did you ask Travis?" I asked, making an attempt to force some life into my voice. She smiled.

"Yeah, I didn't do anything fancy, just asked him after school if he wanted to go, and he said yes. I told him we would be going with you, and he said that sounded good. I still have to ask Mom, but we can figure out the details later when you're feeling better." She was trying to sound casual about it, but there was an undercurrent of excitement in her voice. Still, at the mention of them going to the dance with me, I groaned. She seemed not to notice. She just closed the door softly and left me to my misery again.

Now I had made Corrie mad at me, and I was still expected to go to the dance. I didn't remember going the first time around. Would it mess everything up for me to go now? More of those same questions I couldn't answer. Finally I put on my headphones and turned on the radio, hoping to drown them out at least for a little while.

Chapter
19

Mitch had never had a girlfriend before he met me. In fact, he'd had almost no experience with girls at all. He'd always been too shy to approach them and too clueless to realize when they were approaching him. As for me, I had spent my entire life up to that point obsessing over Sam. It had made for a very short conversation when we had the "previous relationships" talk. Neither of us ever felt the lack, though. We were both happy. Sometimes the guys at work would tease Mitch about how he had never played the field. He would come home and tell me what they had said and laugh about how pitiful they were. To both of us there had never been a reason to play the field when we'd already hit a home run.

Every once in a while, though, usually on really bad days when I felt that I was fat or ugly or was grumpy from being up all night with a baby, I'd wonder if he loved me because I really was the right person for him or if I was just convenient. On rotten days like those, he would invariably sense that something was wrong. I don't know how he did it, but those were the days that he would wrap me in his arms and tell me how beautiful I was and how lucky he was to be with someone like me. I never felt safer, more accepted for who I was, than at those times. That was the magic of Mitch.

When I woke a little after midnight, it was the need for comfort like that of Mitch's loving arms that drove me out of bed. I wrapped up in my thick robe, grateful that the worst of the shivering seemed to have passed, and went to the kitchen. As usual, moments after I started making a snack, Dad, the chronically light sleeper, appeared. He sat down on a barstool at the counter and watched quietly as I made toast and spread peanut butter thickly on each piece. I poured a glass of chocolate milk for each of us and carried the plates over to him. It was this silent camaraderie as much as the physical comfort of the food and my dad sitting near me that started to soothe my fears.

"That was perfect, just what I needed," Dad said when we had finished. He got up to clear the dishes. I watched as he quietly washed them, but I noticed that his eyes drifted toward me occasionally, examining me. "I imagine you were pretty hungry, too, after missing dinner tonight. Right?" I smiled in response. He was so transparent.

"A little," I said. Dad dried the dishes carefully, resting a plate on the counter and wiping off one side, then turning it over to finish it. Everything he did took extra steps and creativity just to complete the same task that others took for granted. He didn't complain—in fact he insisted on being allowed to participate in the daily work of life. Watching him deliberately and expertly maneuver through the simple task was therapeutic. It put things in perspective.

Just as he was finishing and preparing to go back upstairs, I took a leap of faith.

"Dad, can we talk for a minute?" I asked. My voice sounded too loud in the quiet kitchen. Dad stopped and came back to sit by my side.

"What's up, baby cakes?" he asked gently. I hesitated, wanting to phrase things in just the right way.

"Things are just really hard. I can't really explain it all, but I feel like everything I do is taking me farther and farther away from where I need to be in life. I want to have certain things happen, well, I kind of *know* what needs to happen, but I'm just not sure if I'm doing what I should be doing to get there." I blew out a frustrated breath. "It sounds lame when I say it out loud, Dad, but just trust me. Everything is pretty messed up right now." I dropped my head onto my folded arms.

Dad reached over and rubbed my back, his warm hand comforting me. He was quiet, but I knew it just meant he was thinking.

"Did I ever tell you about the first day I saw your mother?" he asked unexpectedly. I sat up straighter and considered the question.

"Sure, when Uncle Teddy and Aunt Joan introduced you at their wedding, right?" I responded, wondering what this had to do with my question.

"No. That was the first time I *talked* to her, but the first time I saw her was about three years earlier. I was at the library going through the paper, trying to find a job. I'd been home for only about six weeks, and I was still pretty darn self-conscious about walking around with only one arm. Mary came in to study with a couple of her roommates, and she was the most beautiful thing I had ever seen. I must have watched her for an hour or more. They were smiling and laughing—they got in trouble with the librarian once. She was just so carefree and . . ." He struggled for the right word. " . . . captivating. I wanted to go talk to her real bad, but I didn't have the nerve. I had just spent the last eighteen months in some of the most terrifying situations any human could face, but that pretty girl in the library was the scariest thing I had ever seen. In the end I chickened out. I started to walk over to her, but instead my legs took me right out the door and into my car and all the way home.

"For the next three years I'd find myself thinking about her at odd moments, and twice more I caught a glimpse of her, both times with that Jeffrey fellow she was seeing." He stood up and started to turn off the lights.

"Dad, don't leave me hanging like that. What happened?" I asked.

"Well, when I saw her at Joan and Teddy's wedding and she was there without Jeffrey, I asked around. Joan told me that they weren't together anymore, and I decided that this was my chance. I wasn't going to let it pass me by one more time. I asked her to dance, and, lo and behold, she didn't even blink twice at the idea of dancing with a one-armed man."

I thought about the pictures from my parents' wedding, Mom with her hair long and straight, looking like the quintessential hippie, and

Dad with his huge sideburns and burly build, grinning from ear to ear in every picture.

"Well, who wouldn't want to dance with you, Dad?" I joked. He didn't laugh, though.

"Plenty of girls, actually. You've grown up with me in your life, so people who are hurt or different are just people to you, but most people don't know how to handle someone who is different. That was one of the most beautiful things about your mother. Still is, in fact." I thought about what he was saying and nodded.

"I guess I just can't imagine anyone not wanting to be with you, Dad," I said. "Look, I think I get what you are saying about not letting chances slip by you, but I'm just not sure what to do with that. My problem is that I'm afraid those chances may have already disappeared and that every choice is taking them farther and farther away, more and more out of my control." The frustration and fear swept back in again, and I sighed under the weight.

"Well, Annie Bell, that wasn't really the point I was trying to make. This is the great adventure of your life. You can't always control it, and you can't do it perfectly. You do your best and you live, and that is all you can do. Sometimes things go wrong. Sometimes you will make decisions that you regret, but one thing will never serve you and that is facing life from a place of fear. Fear won't ever get you anywhere, baby cakes. Fear will hold you back and keep you from choosing, and when you are stuck like that, life just becomes something that happens to you. 'Today is the first day of the rest of your life.'" He delivered this favorite line with a straight face, one that I couldn't quite mirror.

"I know you and your mother like to laugh at me, and that's okay, but it's that line that haunted me in a big way when I first got injured. If today was the first day of the rest of my life, then I wasn't sure I wanted to keep living. Then one day they brought in a guy who had been scouting out land mines in a rice paddy, and he had lost both legs and an arm. He was so happy to have survived so he could go home to his sweetheart that I felt like a whiny little boy for all the moping

I'd been doing. I decided that I was going to live my life and enjoy it, too. There's no point in living if you're not enjoying it." He took a step forward and reached out his arm to wrap it around me in that comforting, lopsided bear hug of his.

"Annie, listen to me, okay?" he asked, leaning back to catch my eye until I nodded. "You are a beautiful girl, and you have so much going for you. You've got family and friends and people all around you who love you. You care about people . . ." He paused as that brought the tears to my eyes.

"No, I don't, Daddy," I sniffed, slipping unconsciously back into that name I hadn't used since I was ten or so. "I'm selfish. I only think about what I want, and I hurt people." I cried harder, thinking of Sam and Corrie and Hannah. My parents.

"That is not true. You are a kid, kiddo, in case you've forgotten, and sometimes you are going to do stupid things, but don't let that make you doubt who you really are inside. Your problem isn't that you don't care about other people. It's that you don't care enough for yourself. Think about it, Annie. What is the last thing you did that made you truly joyful? You've got to find a way to stop worrying about everyone else. You can't control that. Just find that joy and then find a way to share it with someone else, and you'll discover that things will start to sort themselves out. And remember, just like with your mother and me, sometimes it's not the person or the opportunity that is wrong but just the timing. Things always work out the way they are supposed to as long as you are willing to try again and give it time." Dad squeezed me tight again and kissed me on the top of my head before ushering me up the stairs, clicking the light off behind him.

Chapter
20

What made me joyful? I asked myself that question for the hundredth time since my conversation with Dad the night before. I stared out of the window in the front seat as Mom and Hannah chatted about plans for the dance on Friday night. I could feel Mom's eyes on me every few seconds, but I didn't know what to say about the subject.

We pulled up in front of the school, and Hannah practically ran inside. She had biology with Travis first period. I leaned down to grab my bag and my jacket that were on the floor by my feet and then moved to open the door.

"Annie, hold on. Are you sure you feel well enough for school today?" Mom asked. I had to smile at the fact that she would ask such a question. It had always been me trying to get out of school and Mom seeing through me and making me go anyway. Now it was the opposite.

"I'm fine," I lied. What else was I going to do? Lie in bed and feel sorry for myself? I was still exhausted and the thought was tempting, but I was desperately clinging to the hope that I had been sent here for a reason and that if I could discover that reason, then I could get home to my kids. Staying in bed didn't seem to fit in with that idea.

Mom reached out her hand and placed it on my forehead, then my cheek and neck, checking for fever. Her eyes were filled with concern.

"Okay, well, call me if you start to feel sick again. I should be home most of the day," she said.

I gave her what I hoped was a reassuring smile and nodded. Then I got out and walked toward the school.

I quickly failed my English test, along with at least half of the rest of the class. It took a lot of self-control to keep from having negative thoughts about Mrs. Crayk for her use of sarcasm and insults to try to "encourage" her students to do better next time. Next I endured chemistry, happy in this one instance to be one of the less attractive girls in the room, thus avoiding the ogling that other girls were subjected to in Mr. Hanover's class. It was an amazing relief to be freed from that class for lunch break. No wonder teenagers were so messed up all the time.

I walked into the cafeteria and got in line, scanning the crowd for Corrie. Hannah came in with Travis and her other friends, and I smiled at the buoyant expression on her face. By the time I got my food I still hadn't seen Corrie. I stood still for a moment, scanning the room. She wasn't at our usual table or anywhere else. I found an empty seat in the corner and stared at my salad in disgust. She was probably avoiding me.

The chair across from me scraped, and I glanced up in surprise as Sam sat down, plopping his tray on the table.

"Where is Corrie?" he asked.

"That's what I was wondering. We had a bit of a fight yesterday," I said.

He didn't eat, just stared at me with his arms folded across his chest. What was he thinking? I wasn't sure if I was ready to have a conversation with him yet. I was still too confused about what he'd said the day before. I wanted to be with Mitch. Mitch was my husband, the father of my children, the man I loved more than anything in the world, but there was still that part of me, small though it might be, that had been playing his words over and over again with relish. Even with all the fear of the unknown, the pain of missing my kids and the longing to be with Mitch, that part of me was filled with joy that Sam had said he wanted to be with me.

The rest of me was very, very angry with that other part and took it out on Sam.

"Did you want something?" I asked rudely.

"Yes," he said. There was a pause as I waited for him to explain.

"Well?" I finally prompted. "What?" I crossed my arms, mirroring his posture.

He laughed. "You're in a bad mood," he said, grinning.

"And . . . ?" I asked again.

"Nothing. It's just encouraging," he said. He leaned forward and took a big bite of his sandwich. I glared at him.

"Why is my bad mood encouraging to you?" I asked.

He continued to chew, pointing to his mouth and holding up a finger for me to wait. He swallowed before taking a long drink of his soda.

"It just is. You wouldn't be in such a bad mood if things were going well with Mitch. So, you know, that just makes my day." He grinned and continued eating.

I groaned and dropped my head onto my folded arms on the table.

"What are you mumbling?" Sam asked.

I lifted up my head and glared at him again.

"I said, why do you have to make everything so hard?" I asked.

He laughed. "Really? *You* are really asking me that? Let's consider, shall we? You've had, by your own admission, a crush on me since you were twelve, but you never once told me until Sunday with that note. Now that I know and I'm telling you that I return the sentiment, you are too busy chasing after a twenty-three-year-old man that you haven't ever met, and *I'm* the one making things difficult?"

He leaned back against the chair again and smiled smugly. I considered his description. It was depressingly accurate. The whole thing sounded ridiculous. I knew that. But to have him put it all together like that? I had to admit it was a little funny.

"You're right," I said, unable to hold back a smile. "I *am* making things difficult, but it's just that I don't have a choice. It's complicated."

"You've said that before, but, complicated or not, you always have a choice," he answered, and the intensity was back.

"How do you do that?" I asked abruptly.

"What?"

"That thing with the eyes. If you wouldn't do that, it would sure make my life a lot easier," I grumbled, picking up my fork and stabbing a piece of lettuce.

"What thing with my eyes?" he asked, staring deeply at me. I couldn't look away, and I shivered as a chill ran up and down my arms. He noticed the shiver and laughed.

"Stop it," I grumbled, but I had to laugh, too. This was a new, playful side of Sam that I hadn't seen much of. It made him even more attractive than he usually was. As far as I was concerned, that was really saying something. We both ate in silence for a minute, or at least he ate and I picked at my food.

"So why the fight?" he asked after he swallowed.

"What fight?"

"With Corrie. You said you'd had a fight. I thought you two were inseparable. What happened?" he asked.

"I don't want to talk about it. Not today. Anyway, she's probably right about everything, so I don't blame her for being mad."

Surprisingly, Sam let it go. He finished his soda and leaned back with a smile.

"Orchestra today. What are we going to tell Mr. Allan? We never went through that sonata," he said.

"Wait—I thought you didn't want to do it?" I said in surprise.

"I changed my mind. I changed my mind about a couple of things, actually," he said.

"Dare I ask?" Even as I spoke it occurred to me that I was falling into the trap of being too interested in this conversation. I should just get up and leave.

I stayed.

"I've decided that I fit into your life perfectly," he said. Then he got up and left the table, emptying his tray on the way out the door.

I shut my mouth and hurried after him. A large group of sopho-mores left their table at the same time, and I got held up as they all crowded around the garbage can. Finally I just left my tray on a table and walked out. I caught up with Sam outside the door to our class. This seemed to be becoming a habit.

"Why do you do that?" I asked, all of my irritation from earlier returning full force. "What is it about you that feels the need for the dramatic exit? When you drop a bombshell like that, or like yesterday, the least you could do is stick around and explain it so that I don't lie awake at night wondering what it is that you mean. Seriously! Men talk about women being hint droppers. You take being cryptic to a whole new level."

Sam leaned against the wall next to the door with his arms crossed, looking casual and relaxed as I berated him.

"How was I being cryptic?" he asked. "I told you yesterday that I felt like it would just never work out, so I had never considered us together. Well, I've been spending this week doing a lot of considering, and the more I think about it, the more I realize that you are exactly what I want. I'm sorry if I tend to be dramatic. I guess it's the musician in me, wanting a big finish or something." He grinned, pleased with his analogy. I gritted my teeth. I was messing everything up, and I was starting to feel another bout of tears coming on. I couldn't handle any more.

"Sam. I. Can't. Do. This," I said quietly, emphasizing every word. "Listen, the first time around I would have welcomed the idea of you and me with open arms. It was the only thing I could think about. But now it's different. I mean, I'm still totally attracted to you, which is probably illegal, all things considered, but I have my kids to think about. I have a life, and it's a really good life, and if I let myself fall in love with you again, then what happens to them? What about my husband? I mean, I know he's dead, but now he's not, and it's all just so confusing without you telling me you want to be with me. Why couldn't you have done this the first time?"

I saw the look of complete bafflement on his face and realized what I was saying.

"What are you talking about?" he asked quietly. I stared at him for a long time. He was confused, but he also seemed worried. "Please, Annie, tell me what is going on?"

"I can't. You wouldn't believe me. No one would. I don't even believe me," I said.

A couple of kids turned the corner and headed toward us. Sam looked up at them and then back at me, considering.

"Come with me," he said suddenly. He grabbed my hand and pulled me down the hall, away from the classroom and toward the stage. I followed him, wishing I didn't like the feel of his fingers so much.

Chapter
21

*S*am pushed open the door to the stairs that led backstage. It was nearly pitch black with just a hint of green light coming from the exit sign above the doors that led to the parking lot. Sam led me over to the back corner and made me sit on a pile of wood pallets, then leaned over to flick on a small work light. I had been back here only during the musical the year before and never for more than just a few moments. Sam saw me glancing around.

"Sometimes I come here when I need a quiet place to think. It's usually deserted unless there is a show going on." He sat down next to me. "Now, tell me what is going on."

I shook my head mutely.

"Listen, I've told you things that I've never told anyone else. I told you about that time Leonard beat up my mom and about my dad leaving and all of that garbage. Now it's your turn. Something happened to you, and I want to know what it is. Maybe I can help."

I laughed at that idea. "That would be a miracle," I said. "Besides, like I said, there is no way that I can explain it. You won't believe me."

"Try me." He reached out and took my hand again, and I let him. I let him hold my hand, and I started to cry because it felt so nice. It had been so long since I had felt anything like this. I felt like a traitor, like I was betraying Mitch, and yet I didn't want to take my hand away.

"Annie, whatever it is, it can be fixed. Let me help you work it out," he said, rubbing my hand gently. I just cried even harder. Sam pulled me against him until my head was resting on his shoulder and his arm was wrapped around me. He rubbed my back and let me cry.

He smelled so good, and his arm felt so comforting around me. I had to pull myself together and lean away from him before I did something really stupid.

I sat up and wiped my eyes, grateful for waterproof mascara.

"This is really getting to be a habit," I said, trying to lighten the mood.

"I hate that. I didn't mean to make you cry," he said.

"It's not your fault. Well, not entirely," I said. "It's just . . ." My voice faded. How could I possibly describe it?

"Complicated?" he asked. "Yes. You mentioned that once or twice. Well, what is so complicated?"

"Sam, I really appreciate that you want to help me, but there is nothing that you can do. I don't know if there is anything that anyone can do." I covered my face with my hands in defeat. Sam got up and paced the small corner that was illuminated by the lamp. I could hear his footsteps creaking across the wooden floor. Back and forth. Back and forth. His pace was increasing. I looked up and was surprised to see that his hands were clenched and his teeth gritted in anger. I wondered what had suddenly made him so furious. All of a sudden he stopped in front of me and crouched down so he could look at my face.

"Have you told your parents yet?" he finally asked, sadness laced through every word.

"I haven't told anyone. I can't. I don't know what it would mean if I did, but it's definitely not something they would understand. I just have to figure this out on my own," I said.

He shook his head.

"You have to tell them. They'll understand. I know they're strict, especially your mom, but they love you. They'll help you to figure out what to do. You have choices, you know." He was trying to be encouraging, but the comforting words couldn't mask the rage boiling just under the surface. Suspicion flared in me.

"Sam? What are you talking about?"

"Come on, Annie, it's obvious, I don't know why I didn't figure it out before. You're pregnant, right? This guy, this *Mitch*," he spat the name out with disgust, "got you pregnant, and now he's leaving you to deal with it. You said something about taking care of your kid—that's what's going on here, isn't it?"

He stopped talking abruptly as I let out a loud laugh. I clapped my hand over my mouth, but I couldn't stop laughing. The look of confusion on his face made it worse. The idea of my being pregnant was just so far from the truth that I couldn't contain my amusement. Sam sank down onto the floor and watched me laugh with a bemused expression on his face.

"I take it that's not it, then?" he asked, looking so embarrassed that it set me off again. I shook my head, laughing too hard to speak. Finally, when I was able to breathe, I smiled at him.

"I'm not pregnant. Not even close. No. My problem is that I'm from the future." The words sounded so funny, something from a bad '80s science fiction movie, that I started laughing again. I could tell he was disgusted by my apparently joking around when I had been so seriously upset just moments before.

"Fine," he said. "Don't tell me. But you need to talk to someone." He got up to leave, and the laughter died away. He needed to understand. Everything poured out of me in a rush.

"Sam, don't leave. I know it sounds crazy, and I don't expect anyone to believe me, least of all you, but it's true. I'm thirty-eight years old. I have three kids. Mallory is eleven. Jenna is seven, almost eight, and James will be two in December.

"I grew up, Sam. I've done this all before. I finished high school and went to college and met Mitch and we got married and had kids and bought a house. I did all of those things that you talked about yesterday. I am that mom who cooks dinner and drives carpool and does laundry. But then Mitch died." I paused as the tears pricked behind my eyes. My voice cracked, and I cleared my throat. "He died two and a half years ago of a brain aneurysm. It happened out of the blue. He was in a coma for three days, and then he was gone. He never woke up, and I didn't get to say good-bye. He was there, alive and breathing and laughing at a joke Mallory had just told us, and then he walked outside to mow the lawn. The next thing I knew, he was lying on the ground. And it's been really, really hard. I can barely stand it. I try to keep it all together for the girls and James, but I'm failing. I just kind of gave up on life. I take care of my kids, though. You need to know that. They mean everything to me. They are the only thing that matters now, but I don't know how to be happy anymore. It's like that part of me is dead, too." I kept going, unable to stop the words that were pouring out of me.

"I came to stay with my parents and I was sleeping in my old bedroom and when I woke up in the morning I was here. I was sixteen again. Look, I know it sounds crazy. Believe me, I know, but here I am.

"And if I mess this up, if I make the wrong choices, then I'll never marry Mitch and I'll never see my kids again." Saying those words out loud, my fears about my children, brought them back with such force it felt like all of my air was being sucked out. "Oh, Sam. What if I never see them again?" I wrapped my arms around myself and tried hard to keep breathing. Sam was still standing, rooted to the spot, staring at me. I drew in a ragged breath, then another, until I was able to regain my voice.

"It's okay. I told you that you wouldn't believe me. I really don't expect you to." He walked back slowly and knelt in front of me. Contrary to my words, I desperately wanted him to believe me. I tried to dredge up any memory I could find that might convince him I was telling the truth. Something occurred to me, and I sat up straighter.

"Sam, you wrote a song. It was called 'Small Town Girl,' and it was for your mom. You played it at the Winterfest concert." He blinked at me in surprise.

"How do you know about that song?" he asked. "I just started it."

"Because I was there when you performed it. It was this year, and it was the most beautiful thing I'd ever heard. I tried to tell you that I loved it, but I didn't get a chance. You left with Miranda right after the concert, and then you went to visit your dad in San Jose and you never came back to school. I wrote to you nearly every day, trying to convince you to come home, or at least to keep up with your music, and sometimes you wrote back. I saved every letter. Then one day during the next summer you showed up on my doorstep again, and you said that you appreciated all the letters but that you had a girlfriend and she was getting suspicious. So I stopped writing, and we saw each other only once or twice a year when you came to visit your mom and she dragged you to church.

"She kept me up to date on your life, though. You lived with a couple of different girlfriends, and then you joined the Air Force, and I started to write to you again. That's when the phone calls started. Whenever you could, you called me, and we talked for hours, running up huge phone bills, and I started to hope again.

"Then one day you showed up at church. You were waiting in the parking lot, and I was so ecstatic. I just knew that you were there, after all these years, to tell me you loved me. You asked me to walk with you for a minute, and I followed, gladly. You took me to your car and introduced me to the girl who was waiting inside. She was your fiancée, Savannah.

"I was heartbroken. I thought I'd understood what that felt like before, but this was worse—it was so final. I finally had to admit, after all those years, that you were never going to love me.

"I met Mitch just a few weeks later, and it was the first time I'd ever been interested in anyone but you. He was the man I was supposed to be with. And now he's alive. He wouldn't know me from Eve, but he's alive out there, and I miss him so much." I finished with another catch in my throat. Sam continued to stare at me without speaking.

"Please tell me what you are thinking? You think I'm crazy, right? Or making it up, or that I'm delusional. I don't blame you. I would think the same thing if the roles were reversed. It's all true, though. Every word." He was still silent.

"Sam?" I asked quietly. "Do you believe me?"

Chapter

22

I waited for Sam to say something. He stared at me, searching my face for a long moment.

"How did it happen?" he asked finally, his voice very quiet. He didn't say the words, but I could hear something in his voice. Was it really possible that he believed me?

"I don't know. I don't know how to get back, either," I answered. "All I know is that I have to make sure things happen the right way. I can't mess anything up—I can't jeopardize the lives of my kids." He took that in, considering.

"It's not for my mom," Sam said after a minute.

"What?"

"The song, 'Small Town Girl.' I'm not writing it for her. I'm writing it for you," he said.

I searched his face, looking for disgust, or anger, or annoyance. Anything that would say he thought I was crazy. But all I could see was that same Sam intensity.

"Sam," I whispered. "You believe me, don't you?"

"I don't know, Annie. I know you aren't making it up. You obviously believe it, but it's just so far-fetched," he said.

I sighed. "I know. Time travel and all that. It does sound crazy. I thought I was dreaming for a long time. Maybe I am." I sighed again and ran a hand through my hair in frustration.

"Yeah, it's definitely weird. Though I guess some of the things you've been saying lately are making a bit more sense. Still, it all seems really hard to believe, at least what you said about the way I treated you, or that I'm going to treat you, or, well, whatever. Annie, I don't know what happened or how it's all going to work out, but I know one thing. Other than my mom and my music, you are the only thing I care about on this earth."

Warmth spread through me, starting at my heart and working its way out to my limbs.

He continued. "Maybe you're here to do something different. Maybe . . ." He leaned forward slowly, and I realized what he was doing. I knew that it was stupid, but I wanted him to kiss me. His lips looked softer than I had noticed before, and it had been so long since I had felt like anything other than a mom. I wanted this. I wrapped my arms around his neck, and he pulled me closer, his lips just a breath away from mine. For one long, wavering second I let myself consider what it would be like to be wrapped up in the wonderfulness of kissing someone I loved. And I had to admit it to myself: I loved Sam. I had always loved him.

I just loved Mitch more.

I pulled back. "Sam, stop. I'm so sorry. I can't do this. I can't be with you, even though a part of me really wants to. I need to be with him. Mitch is my future and my past," I said, but he was shaking his head.

"He may be your future, but right now you are sixteen years old, and now isn't the time for him. *I'm* here now, and you love me. You've told me so yourself. So why can't we be together at least for now?" He pulled me to him again.

I pushed him away and stood up, walking a few steps to catch my breath. I needed to think, and I couldn't seem to do that with Sam so close to me. I needed space, and I guessed that Sam did, too. Whether he wanted it or not. "I, um, think we should get to class," I finally said.

He sat there on the floor for a few seconds longer and then nodded.

"You're right. We both need to think," he said. He stood up and walked over to me. "Annie, I don't know what is going to happen, but somehow I'm sure that everything is going to work out. You will see your kids again." He smiled, and I felt a tiny bit of hope begin to bloom inside me again at his promise. Whatever else happened, Sam believed me.

Chapter

23

*I*t was amazing, but telling Sam about everything made it seem less impossible. I wasn't bearing the burden of the future alone. He knew my secret, and he believed me. That alone was a miracle. Sam believed me.

It was becoming clear that he loved me, too. That was something I was going to have to face. It was amazing, wonderful, and exhilarating. It was also terrifying. How could I love him and be loved by him in return and still have room in my life, in my future, for Mitch and the kids? I was afraid to see him again, afraid he would want something from me that I couldn't give him. How had everything changed so drastically? What was so different about me now that made Sam love me when he never had before? It seemed too hard to believe that he might always have loved me, not with the way things had gone in my past.

When school got out, I left through a door I rarely took, not going to my locker, even though I had a lot of homework that I really needed to do. I didn't want to see anyone or talk to anyone, especially Sam. Not yet. I walked home, relieved that the day was clear, though it was cold after yesterday's storm.

I needed time to think. I kept telling myself that, but I knew that thinking wasn't really working out very well for me. Last night I had been worried that I was messing everything up. Well, almost kissing Sam, not to mention telling him everything, sure seemed to be pretty high on the list of things that could mess up my future.

"What was I thinking?" I asked myself out loud. I had floated through a haze of dreaminess after that moment with him. Now I was seeing how close I had come to ruining everything. But even now there was part of me that wished I had closed the distance and given in to temptation.

"He's eighteen years old. That is half your age, Annie," I muttered, kicking a loose pebble down the sidewalk. "It might not be illegal, but it's definitely not okay. Not to mention the fact that you're married—well, sort of. You just can't go around kissing Sam. It's a very, very bad idea." *Oh, great,* I thought. *Now I'm talking to myself, too. I'm definitely crazy.*

Maybe that was it. Maybe I was crazy, and this was all just a major hallucination. Sure, a hallucination that had lasted for four days. *That* made sense. I mulled everything over in my mind, a playlist that looped indefinitely as I walked the mile and a half home.

I stopped at the last big intersection before crossing to our neighborhood. There was a small crowd of students on the corner, and I hid in the back of the group when I saw Sam's Honda stop at the light. He started to pull through the intersection when the signal changed, but he stopped quickly as an ambulance came barreling down the street, its siren wailing. I peeked around the burly senior in front of me, wondering what Sam was thinking. Had he missed me after school? I couldn't see his face, though, as he followed the ambulance into our neighborhood, and then made a sharp right turn onto his street.

I walked the last few blocks quickly, just wanting to get home and put this day behind me. I thought about making dinner for my family, longing to lose myself in the process of caring for other people. Maybe I could make enchiladas or Navajo tacos, two of my dad's favorites. I was trying to remember what ingredients had been in the refrigerator and freezer as I turned the corner onto our street and saw that the ambulance from the intersection and a fire engine were parked in front of my house.

My heart stopped. Then it thudded to life painfully as I dashed toward the house, panic welling up inside me. Hannah and Rachel were standing on the front lawn holding hands, and both of them were crying.

"What's going on, Hannah?" I yelled. She just cried harder. I ran in the front door and found Dan sitting on the bottom stair, his head in his hands. He shocked me by running to me and throwing his arms around my waist. Hannah and Rachel came inside at that moment, and all four of us intertwined in a pretzely hug. I instinctively soothed and caressed each of them, trying to offer comfort, but inside I was terrified of what I was going to discover.

I was finally able to disentangle myself and left them all crying in the living room as I made my way fearfully upstairs. Memories of Mitch lying on the ground immobile, the paramedics trying to resuscitate him, rushed over me, and I swallowed down a surge of bile in my throat.

At the top of the stairs, the paramedics were just backing through the door with a stretcher. Mom stood in the hall with her hands over her mouth. Her face was ashen with fear. I followed her gaze to my father's face as he lay strapped to the gurney. His eyes were closed, and his skin was gray. I couldn't tell if he was breathing. I moved out of the way as the paramedics carried him carefully down the stairs.

"Mom?" She turned toward me, and we rushed to embrace. "Is he dead?" I managed to choke out.

"No, honey. He's had a heart attack. We don't know how bad it is. I need to go with him. Please take care of the kids and call Aunt Erin. I'll call you as soon as I have any news." I nodded. She squeezed me tightly once more and followed the gurney out to the ambulance. I gathered up Dan and the girls, and we knelt in the living room and prayed for our father. At least Hannah did, and we listened. I didn't know if I could pray. I tried, but the words stuck in my throat. All I could think was that this hadn't happened the first time around. When I had been a teenager before, Dad had never been ill. Something about my being here was changing things. This was all my fault.

*M*om's sister Erin rushed over as soon as I called her. She wanted to take us all to her house until we knew more. Hannah, Rachel, and Dan all wanted to go, but I refused. I needed to be here where I could help my mom more. I thought at first that Aunt Erin was going to force the issue, but I guess she decided that I was old enough to be on my own, and she left with the other kids, making me promise that I would call her if I changed my mind. As soon as they were gone, I walked through the house, looking for anything that Mom might need while she stayed at the hospital with Dad. I gathered her toothbrush and a hairbrush, her sweater and a book, and then made a couple of sandwiches and packed it all in a tote bag.

I was just pulling out of the garage when Bishop Michaels pulled up in front of the house. I stopped the car and rolled down the window as he walked to my car.

"I just heard about your dad," he said in his most soothing voice. "Any update yet?"

"No," I said. I was a little surprised at how fast he'd heard. "I'm just on my way to the hospital now. I'm sure my mom will call you when we know more."

"Thanks, Annie. I'd appreciate that. And please don't hesitate to let me know if there is anything your family needs. I'll be praying for all of you, especially Hank."

I thanked him and rolled up the window, eager to be away.

I drove to the hospital, gripping the steering wheel so tightly that I lost feeling in my fingers a couple of times. I wanted a cell phone so badly, to be able to call my mother and know what was happening at that minute. The waiting was agonizing.

Why did Dad have a heart attack? What could I have done to bring that on? Was it the late-night snacks I'd been feeding him? That wasn't any different from how things had been before. Was I causing him more stress? I couldn't imagine how. I was being a much nicer person to be around than the old me. Why was this happening? Of course I had no answers to those disturbing questions. I shook my head and tried to focus on driving. Instead I was flooded with those last few memories of Mitch.

That ambulance ride had been torturous. The paramedics were working frantically to stabilize Mitch's vital signs, and I was pushed to the far corner out of the way. I wanted to take his hand and yell at him, to force him to wake up and look at me, but I couldn't make myself move. I stayed frozen in the corner, watching in horror as he remained unresponsive. When we arrived at the hospital, they immediately wheeled him back for an MRI and then into emergency surgery while I was left to fill out the mountain of paperwork. I couldn't understand how they could possibly ask me all those inane questions when Mitch's life was hanging by a thread.

It was the most alone feeling I'd ever had. I had to wait more than two hours before the words "ruptured cerebral aneurysm" explained that it was unlikely that my husband would ever regain consciousness. My mother finally arrived a couple of hours later, and she stayed with me for the rest of the horrific ordeal, but during those first few hours I was all alone.

The nurse directed me to Dad's room, and I paused just outside the door. I could hear the beep of the heart monitor, quiet through the door, and nothing else. The beeping gave me the courage to go inside. Dad was hooked up to all kinds of wires and monitors. His eyes were closed and his face was pale, but his chest rose and fell in a regular rhythm. Mom was sitting at Dad's side, holding his hand. Her eyes were closed, too, but her lips were moving. She was praying. She opened her eyes as I entered, and she blinked in surprise.

"I thought you were at Aunt Erin's," she said.

"The other kids went, but I wanted to bring you this." I handed her the bag I had packed. She glanced inside and then pulled out the sweater with a hint of a grateful smile.

"That's very sweet, honey. Thank you," she said.

I pulled up the other chair and sat down next to her. "How is he?" I asked quietly.

"He's going to be fine. He's just sleeping right now. The drugs are making him drowsy. He had a heart attack, Annie. They are going to be taking him into surgery in about an hour, but the doctor says he thinks it should be pretty straightforward." She sighed and rubbed a hand across her eyes.

"Can I get you anything, Mom?" I asked. "Do you want a soda or a snack or a back rub?" I tried to keep the mood light. Dad was going to be okay. The words were ringing in my ears, but they wouldn't sink into my brain. Still, I needed to be there for my mom. Just as she had been there for me when Mitch died.

"No, I'm okay. Thanks. I think I will slip out for just a minute and run to the restroom. Can you stay here with Dad?" she asked. I nodded and reached out to take his hand. Mom patted my shoulder and left the room, working the kinks out of her shoulders as she walked.

A hospital, a room just like this one, the monitors, the sounds, the smells, the touch of the hand of the man I loved most in the world as he slowly drifted away. It was all too familiar and frightening. No matter what my mom said, as they wheeled Dad away for surgery I was sure I wouldn't see him again.

Mitch's surgery had been brief. There was too much damage. Nothing could be repaired. The surgeon gave me the news as kindly as he could, but there is no easy way to tell someone that her husband is going to die. During the long hours of vigil that followed, my brain and my heart did battle. My mind understood what the doctor had said, knew that there was no way for Mitch to survive with the kind of damage that his brain had experienced. But my heart didn't care about any of that. At first I hoped for him to recover, but as the hours turned into a day and then another, my prayers changed, and I prayed for him to open his eyes, just once, so that I could look into them and tell him I loved him. Tell him good-bye. On the third day, it was obvious that he was drifting away. I prayed harder, but he died at three o'clock in the afternoon. He had never opened his eyes.

When they brought Dad back from surgery, my heart was in my throat. He was so still.

"Mom?" I questioned. She hurried to hug me.

"Don't worry—he's just coming out of the anesthesia. The doctor said everything went really well. He'll wake up before too long."

I nodded, allowing her words and her touch to soothe me. I knew this wasn't the same as it was with Mitch. I needed to hold it together. Still, when Dad finally blinked and asked for Mom, all the fear that I had been holding at bay threatened to suffocate me, and I had to leave the room. Dad was all right. He was going to live.

Chapter

25

All through the rest of the night and the next day, Mom and I took turns staying by Dad's side. He was uncomfortable and tired very easily, but he was the same old dad. He kept the nurses chuckling with one-armed man jokes and teased Mom mercilessly whenever she pressured him to rest. It was comforting to see him so restored to his old self, and Mom finally persuaded me to go home and get a few hours of sleep. As I drove I realized with a start that it was Friday night. Hannah had missed the dance, and I had no idea what had happened with Corrie. All of the angst and stress over the dance had been for nothing. In the end the choice had been taken from my hands anyway. Even thinking about the dance while my dad lay in the hospital had seemed small and ludicrous.

I was back at the hospital first thing in the morning to spell Mom off. She went home to shower and to go check on the kids at Aunt Erin's. Dad was sleeping, so I lay down on the cot Mom had been using and tried to doze again. I was startled awake when Dad spoke my name.

"Annie, help me, please," he said breathlessly. I jumped to my feet, afraid that he was in pain, but he was just trying to change positions, which was a struggle with only one hand to maneuver. I helped him to shift in the bed and adjusted his bedding. He sighed in satisfaction and settled back against the pillows.

"Hand me that water jug?" he asked. I poured him some water and passed it to him. He sipped at it for a moment and then handed the cup back. "So you've been worrying about your old dad, have you?"

"Yes," I said. "You scared me, Dad."

"Well, no harm done. They got me all fixed up, and I'll be back to my usual troublemaking before you know what's what." He tried to sound cheerful, but even the simple act of shifting in bed had left him weak and breathing hard.

"Dad, why did this happen?" I asked. "Was it the peanut butter and toast the other night?" I knew it sounded stupid the moment the words were out, but I didn't know how else to articulate the question. *How did I change things so that this happened to you, Dad? What is it about me that causes this kind of damage?*

"Don't be silly, baby cakes. Things happen for a reason. We don't always know what that reason is, but there is one, just the same." He patted my hand and then reached out and cupped my cheek. "Maybe this happened just so we could spend more time together. I can't think of many things I'd rather do than lie around being waited on by beautiful women."

I smiled at his joke, but inside I was still filled with a desperate sense of responsibility. I was the only thing different this time. I was the part of the equation that had changed. I had to be the cause. Not only did I feel responsible for the pain Dad was experiencing because of me but I was also desperately afraid for the future. Dad smoothed my hair again and searched my eyes. I felt he was seeing through me to the fear and pain in my heart.

"How are you doing, Annie Bell? Other than this old man getting sick and all of that? How are things going for you?"

I shrugged.

"I don't know, Dad. I really don't. I'm trying, though. I remember your advice, and I've been trying to discover what makes me joyful and to be patient and let things work themselves out. I'm trying to figure out what the right choices are, but I just don't know," I said. I was pretty sure he could hear the doubt in my voice that told him I wasn't feeling very successful. Dad gazed off into space for a minute or two. I thought that maybe he was falling back to sleep, but suddenly he began to speak again, his eyes distant.

"One time my squadron was traveling from one village to another in what was supposed to be a clear zone. One minute we were just trudging along, and the next minute we were surrounded by Viet Cong. I was a new sergeant, and I locked up at first. I looked around to try to figure out what to do, and my guys were all looking to me for the answer. I should have signaled retreat and called in an air strike, but every decision seemed worse than the last. It was only a few seconds, but it was the worst fear I had ever felt in my life. No matter which way we turned, we were going to have a fight, and I didn't know what direction to go. So we sat there as crucial seconds ticked by. Next thing I knew, Pete was hit. That shocked me out of it. I called the retreat. I was hit next, but we managed to get out of there with the rest of our guys. I was the lucky one. Pete didn't make it." A flicker of pain crossed his face.

"I'm so sorry, Dad," I said. "I never knew. You never have really talked about it before."

"Well, it's ugly stuff, and I don't want you kids to be thinking about things like that. Still, sometimes I still dream about Pete. He had a wife and a baby back home. He'd never seen his son. It was my job to get my guys out alive, and instead I froze. I let fear paralyze me. That's something I have to live with for the rest of my life." He glanced at my face and must have seen his own pain mirrored there because he smiled and patted my cheek again. "Maybe I shouldn't have told you that, baby cakes. It's a sad, sad story. But the thing is that as sorry as I am for Pete's death, for the death of all of the boys who died in Vietnam, I still have a life, and if I had let myself get caught up in all of that stuff, I wouldn't have your mother or you kids. All of the good things in life come from making those hard choices and from learning to trust people. You can't live your life in fear, Annie. You know, sometimes not making a decision is a decision in and of itself. There can be pain either way. But when you are standing still, you are letting someone else make the choice for you." He closed his eyes again. "Ah, that's a depressing story. Maybe we should watch TV or something so you don't have to listen to me ramble on." His voice was drifting off as the exhaustion hit him full force.

"Thanks, Dad. Thanks for telling me about Pete," I said. "Get some rest now."

The next afternoon, as I left the hospital, I thought about Dad and his story. I knew he meant it to be comforting in some way, to teach me a lesson, and I got what he was trying to say, but it seemed impossible all the same. Just make a decision, huh? Would he have said the same thing if it were Mom or us kids that were hanging in the balance? It was a nice thought, but I didn't really know what to do with it.

I drove slowly, taking backstreets, not really anxious to get home to the empty house. My brain and my hands weren't really connected, and I was a little surprised to find that I had actually taken the turn to go to Mitch's house. Once I realized where I was, I sped up, eager to be there, even just to sit in front of the house.

I pulled up and parked across the street. From my vantage point I could see that the garage door was open. Neither Margaret's sedan nor Charlie's blue truck was there. A thought occurred to me, and I quickly counted the days off on my fingers. I had lost track of how long it had been since Dad's heart attack, but I figured out that today was Sunday. That meant that the Kellys would be at church. I didn't stop to think or consider all the ramifications. I just started the car again and drove to the old white church.

I didn't see Charlie's truck, but a car that I was pretty sure belonged to Margaret was parked in the parking lot. My hands started to shake in anticipation. Mitch never missed church. If Margaret was here, then he was, too. I walked inside quickly, before I could chicken out, and took a seat on the back row. The bishop was speaking, but his words were just white noise in my ears as I scanned the congregation, trying to catch a glimpse of the back of Mitch's head. My heart thudded in my chest as I saw Margaret toward the front of the chapel. She leaned over and whispered something to a tall man next to her. My heart sank in disappointment as he turned to respond to his mother.

Charlie's profile was unmistakable. I searched the rest of the row and craned my neck to look for Mitch in any other part of the congregation. He wasn't there.

I sank back against the bench in frustration. The pinched-faced woman in front of me half turned and glanced in disapproval at my casual clothes and slumped posture. There didn't seem to be any point in my staying, and I was about to get up when something Bishop Jamison was saying bubbled up through my consciousness.

"We are so proud of all of them for their selfless service to those of our Heavenly Father's children who are less fortunate than we are. They are great examples to us all. In fact, Bishop Michaels from the Fourteenth Ward has invited members of the service group to share their experiences in his ward in the hopes that they will inspire their youth in the same way that they have inspired all of us. They are there right now—"

I didn't wait to hear the rest. I hurried back outside to my car.

This was too much, a cruel joke. I vaguely remembered now that all those years ago Bishop Michaels had invited a group to come and speak to us about their service trip. I had been too wrapped up in Sam, sitting one pew in front of me, to pay any attention. Had Mitch actually been in the group? I wouldn't have known him, of course, but it seemed ridiculous to think that I had seen him before and never realized it. If I had been paying attention, I would have known I should be at church today. I drove as fast as I could, but as I watched the clock I already knew that church would be over by the time I got there. I pulled into the half-empty parking lot and scanned the crowd for the truck. It was already gone. I went inside anyway, just to be sure. There were a few people still chatting, but Mitch wasn't there. Bishop Michaels saw me, excused himself from talking to Sister Patrick, and hurried over to me.

"Annie, it's good to see you. How is your father doing? I haven't talked to your mother since yesterday morning."

"He's doing pretty well. They are thinking that he'll still be there for another week or so, as long as there aren't any complications," I said. "Um, bishop, did the service trip group already leave?"

"Oh, you heard about that? Yes, I'm sorry but the last two of them just left. Listen, tell your mom that we want to help out with Thanksgiving this week. A few of the Relief Society sisters have already asked if they could bring over a turkey."

"Oh—thanks, but we are going to my aunt's house for Thanksgiving. She's already got it all arranged," I said. Now that I knew Mitch had left I was eager to be gone.

"Okay, but please tell her just the same. That way she knows her options in case she changes her mind. All right?" he said.

"Sure. And thanks again for everything," I said. I was relieved when he nodded and smiled and then moved to speak to some of the other ward members. I left quickly, disappointment still coursing through me, nearly strong enough to choke me.

Chapter
26

I drove home without really paying attention to what I was doing. I pulled into the garage and slumped over the steering wheel. It seemed like God didn't want me to see Mitch. Was this a punishment, or possibly protection? I had tried to go to his house and missed him by seconds. He'd never responded to the message I had left for him, and now I had missed him again. It was like a practical joke was being played on me, bringing me so close to seeing him and then yanking it all away again.

I dragged myself inside to take a long shower. The hot water washed away some of the weariness but not the sadness. No matter what Dad said, I couldn't see how things would ever come together.

I was getting dressed when the doorbell rang. I finished pulling on a green sweater and hurried down the stairs. I expected it to be the bishop again, or maybe Aunt Erin, but when I opened the door Corrie was standing there.

"Oh, hi," I said. "Come in."

She stepped inside sedately, which was unusual for her. Was she still mad? If the roles had been reversed, I probably would be. She stood there for just a minute, then suddenly burst into tears and threw her arms around me.

"Annie, I'm so sorry. I heard about your dad on Thursday, but I was still so mad at you that I didn't even call to see how you were doing. After Friday I wanted to come see you, but I figured you wouldn't want me here after the way I treated you . . ." She trailed off and broke away.

"The way *you* treated *me*? No way, Corrie," I said. "I'm the one who needs to apologize. I've been really wrapped up in myself lately, and I'm so sorry. I should have made arrangements to be at the dance. I mean, I wouldn't have been able to make it after all, with my dad getting sick, but obviously I didn't know that at the time. At least you would have known how important you are to me. You're my best friend, Corrie. I'll never have another friend like you." It was the truth. She might be a little too bouncy sometimes, but she was one person that seemed to understand me. I had really missed that as an adult. I'd really missed *her*.

"Of course you won't." She smiled. "Why would you need one? We'll be friends forever, anyway."

I wasn't quite sure what to say, so I just nodded. I invited her into the kitchen, and we dug through the refrigerator until we found something to eat. While we made grilled cheese sandwiches and tomato soup, I told her about my dad and his surgery. She listened and made all the usual sympathetic noises at the right moments. I couldn't help but wonder what had happened on Friday night. She seemed so normal, not at all like someone who had been molested by her boyfriend. Finally I had to bring it up.

"How did things go on Friday with Jesse, anyway?" I asked as we sat down at the counter with our food.

"Ugh, it was awful," she said. I cringed. "You were right—about everything. Jesse was a total scumbag, to put it mildly."

"What happened?"

"I *so* don't want to talk about it. Let's just say that he tried to push things too far, and I wasn't interested. He was so rude. I don't know why I didn't see it before. I mean, he's always been kind of pushy. Still, I just kept hearing you call him a jerk. It was like you were there whispering it in my ear, and finally it just hit me—yeah, he *is* a jerk. I deserve better than that." Taking a big bite of her sandwich, she continued talking with her mouth full. "So I punched him in the face."

"What?" I asked, choking on my soup and sputtering in surprise. She grinned and pounded me on the back, enjoying my shock.

"I know, right? But I did. I totally punched him in the face. You should have seen him. He acted like a baby about it, too." She took another bite and chewed for a minute, suddenly subdued. "Apparently he told Angela and Andrew that I—well, you can imagine what he said. He's a *total* jerk. I wish I'd punched him twice," she muttered.

"Wow, Corrie. I am so sorry. You did the right thing, though, and you *do* deserve so much better than that."

I leaned over and hugged her. When she pulled away, there was a hint of a tear in her eye. She blinked it away and smiled again.

"I am *not* going to cry over him," she insisted.

"Good for you."

We finished our lunch, chatting about school and the other kids she had seen at the dance. After we did the dishes, I roped Corrie into doing the grocery shopping with me. We cleaned the house, and the work was so much lighter with a friend helping. It was a great afternoon. Corrie's lighthearted chatter and the fact that we were doing something for my mom left me feeling happier than I'd been since Dad's heart attack. I finished dusting, Corrie put away the vacuum, and we flopped on the living room couch.

"Do you want some ice cream?" I asked. "My dad always has some in the freezer."

"Mmmm, tempting, but I have to get going. I still have so much homework to do," she said. "By the way, Mr. Allan asked about you on Friday. He was talking to Sam about some duet. Sam told him that he didn't think you were going to be able to manage it, with your dad being sick and all. I tried asking him about it today, but he just changed the subject. What duet were they talking about?"

"When did you talk to Sam?" I asked, ignoring her question in my surprise. They normally only associated with each other in the brief moments that we were all together.

"He called right after he got home from church, I guess. It was weird, actually. I didn't even know he had my number." A flame of jealousy flared up in me. Sam had called her?

"School directory?" I suggested, trying to keep my voice even.

Corrie took one look at my face and laughed. It must not have been as carefully controlled as I thought.

"Don't look at me like that. He called me to talk about you, after all. He said you really wanted to see me and that I should call you. I already wanted to come over, but, you know, I wasn't sure if I should. After I talked to him, I decided to just do it."

"Well, I'm really glad you did." Inside I was reeling. What had made Sam do that? How did he know that Corrie was exactly what I needed today?

"Yeah, me, too." She bounced up off the couch and grabbed her jacket from the back of the chair. "Well, I'll see you tomorrow. Do you want a ride to school?"

"No, I still have my dad's car. I have to go pick up my brother and sisters from my aunt's tonight anyway." I walked with her to the door. School loomed before me again. Even though worrying about my dad was stressful, it had been a nice break from thinking about school. Schoolwork, school drama—it took a lot of energy. I sighed.

Corrie understood instantly, as she usually did. "Well, at least it's a short week."

I nodded, then hugged her again. "Thanks for today, Corrie. You're the best. Literally," I said.

"I know, right?" She laughed as she bounded down the walk to her car. I watched her go and then closed the door when she pulled away.

Once again something had changed, but this time it was good. Corrie had finally seen through Jesse. Instead of being assaulted by him, putting up with it, and letting him ruin her life, she had punched him in the face. I pictured tiny Corrie hitting Jesse, nearly six feet tall and built like Arnold Schwarzenegger, and I had to laugh. It could have been so much worse—had been at one point, in fact. But she'd broken free from him. She was going to have to deal with some nasty rumors thanks to Jesse's horrid comments and Angela's big mouth. Still, she could handle it. We would handle it together.

Chapter

27

I needed to pick up Hannah, Dan, and Rachel, but I still had a couple of hours, and there was someone else I needed to see first.

As I walked to Sam's house, I tried to compose a carefully worded statement that would include everything that I needed to say. No emotion. Just the facts. He had become the rock I had grown to depend on during the past week. He had driven me to Mitch's house, something that I was only now realizing I had really needed. He had listened to me whine and cry, and, amazingly, he'd believed me when he should have dismissed me as a lunatic. On top of all that, he had sent Corrie my way today, something I would be forever grateful for. I owed him my thanks for everything he had done for me. But would I get distracted once I was with him? That's what seemed to happen every time. The last thing I needed was to break my promise to myself and kiss him—as if things weren't already complicated enough.

By the time I got to his door, I still hadn't figured out everything I wanted to say, but I took a deep breath and rang the bell anyway. I heard the TV playing inside, but it was silenced when the bell chimed. A few seconds later Alice Sharp answered the door. She was a small, thin woman with a perpetually wary look on her face. According to Sam, this cautiousness was a holdover from her first marriage to Sam's father, even before she had met Leonard. When she saw me at the door, a smile lit up her face. I remembered this reaction from my first time around. For some reason that I had never quite understood, Sister Sharp really liked me. A couple of years after I was married, she had finally divorced Brother Sharp and moved away. I had been happy for her, but I missed seeing her whenever I visited our old ward with my family.

"Annie, come in. How is your father doing?" she asked as she ushered me inside. I answered her inquiries about my father with a smile, but I entered the house nervously, not wanting to encounter Leonard and all of his false joviality. Even if Sam hadn't told me about Leonard's abusive treatment, I would have known something was off. He had always rubbed me the wrong way. Thankfully, Sister Sharp's next words put my mind at ease, at least on that score.

"My husband is out for the evening," she said. "Sam just got back, though. I'll go and get him."

"It's okay, Mom," Sam said from the doorway to the hall. "I heard the bell." He stood just inside the door and leaned against the wall, his hands in his pockets. Sister Sharp smiled up at him, murmured something about dinner, and went into the kitchen, leaving us alone. I felt suddenly shy in his presence. I sank down on the couch and looked down at my hands. I suddenly realized that I wasn't wearing my wedding ring. Not only had my children disappeared from this world but every physical reminder of my life, all of my pictures and keepsakes, were gone, not created yet. It was a sobering thought.

The silence stretched on, and I finally had to look up to try to see what Sam was thinking. He wasn't looking at me but was staring out the window at the remains of another beautiful autumn day. His dark eyes seemed sad, older than his years, and I found myself wanting to make that sorrow disappear. The moment was brief, though, and that look was replaced by a mischievous one as he recognized that I was staring.

"Well? What's the verdict?" he asked. "Have you figured me out yet?"

"Hardly. I was just thinking that you don't seem eighteen," I said with a smile.

"Neither do you," he said.

"Well, that's because I'm not eighteen. Remember? I'm thirty-eight."

"No, you aren't. You're sixteen," he argued with just a touch of a frown.

"Well, whatever. That's beside the point. You always seemed so much older than the other kids at school," I said. *Focus,* I told myself. *Don't get distracted.* I changed the subject.

"I wanted to thank you for everything this last week. It's been hard, but you've been there for me. I just want you to know that I've appreciated all of it. Especially today with Corrie. I don't know how you knew to call her, but it was exactly what I needed." I rushed through the words.

"It's no problem," he said dismissively. His nearness to me on the sofa ignited that electric spark again, but I squelched it and scooted a couple of inches away. *Focus,* I reminded myself.

"Well, I just . . . anyway, thanks." We were both silent again for a moment, and this time I could feel Sam's eyes on me.

"I met Mitch today," he said.

I jumped a little at the name, and my eyes flew to his face. "Really? At church? What happened?" I asked.

"Yeah, at church. He's freakishly tall, you know," he said.

I laughed at the description. "I know. Six-six, actually. Mallory and Jenna both have those genes. I'm not sure yet, but I think that James will, too," I said with a smile, but it quickly faded. I rubbed at my naked ring finger. Thinking about them always hurt.

"You miss them." It wasn't a question.

"You have no idea." My voice cracked, and I swallowed, trying to push down the lump in my throat.

I looked up at him. He was studying me with that intense look that always made me feel defenseless. "What are you thinking, Sam? I mean, how can you take all of this in and just accept it? I wouldn't if it weren't happening to me." Sam shrugged and smiled.

"This may come as a shock to your system, but I'm actually pretty observant," he said.

I laughed at that, wondering how he could claim that trait when he hadn't noticed I'd been following him like a puppy for the last four years.

He caught my meaning. "I know, I guess I do have a couple of blind spots. Still, you were one person on Sunday, and on Monday you were someone different. You were still you, but you had changed so dramatically. When you told me that you grew up, it made sense. I mean, the whole thing doesn't make sense at all, but that one statement does. I guess it makes as good sense as anything else in life. The thing is, Annie, I trust you. You've never looked at me with disgust or judgment, like everyone else does. You've always just accepted me, and I owe you the same courtesy."

It was such a straight answer, so unexpected after all of his cryptic remarks in the past, that I was completely captivated. In that moment I almost broke my rule. He was so close. It would be so easy to kiss him. I saw in his face that I wouldn't have to do anything other than let it happen. He wanted it, too. But I wouldn't cross that line.

I sat up a little straighter, putting another inch or two between us. "Thanks, Sam. It's the most wonderful thing to have someone I can talk to who knows what's really going on. And now you've met Mitch! Tell me—what happened? Did you talk to him? What did he say?"

Sam's eyes were disappointed for just a moment, but he quickly hid that emotion and smiled. "I talked to him. He complimented me on the music, and I told him that I enjoyed hearing about his trip."

I could picture the two men talking, facing each other, one tall and blond with piercing blue eyes, the other dark and a little shorter and more muscled. The image flared in my mind, the two men that I loved standing face to face. I hadn't seen it with my own eyes, but it was burned in my brain anyway.

"It sounds very civil," I finally said after clearing my throat. Sam grinned.

"Yep, very civil. He really does seem like a good guy. Way too tall and too old for you, of course, but a good guy all the same." His words warmed me.

"He really is, Sam. You need to know that. He's a really good man. Thanks for telling me." I was quiet for a minute. "Well, at least *you've* seen him. I can't seem to make that happen. I kind of feel like 'three strikes and you're out,' you know?"

"Maybe the time just isn't right. Have you thought about that?" he asked.

"I guess. Maybe you're right. In any case, I don't see it happening in the next couple of days. Not with me watching my sisters and brother, visiting my dad, taking care of the house, and practicing our sonata."

"Are you still planning on that? I figured it wouldn't work with your dad being sick," he said.

"I want to, Sam. I think that it's exactly what I need. My dad is always telling me to do things that make me feel joyful, and music is all I can think of. I'd like to play it—you know, for my dad."

He considered that for a moment, and I thought I saw something flicker in his eyes. Could it have been excitement? Whatever it was, he was careful to sound nonchalant when he answered.

"Well, if that is what you want, then let's do it. I've been running through it, actually, and it's really beautiful."

"Great! I've played it through only a couple of times, but I think I can manage. Can we practice at my house? It'll be easier, with me babysitting and all that. After school?" I asked. Sam nodded, and I smiled in return. "Excellent. Well, I need to go. I'm picking up the kids tonight from my aunt's house."

"That's probably for the best, anyway," Sam said. "Leonard will be home soon, and it'll be easier that way."

We both stood, and he walked me to the door, but I couldn't leave yet. I hesitated for just a moment, afraid to trust my own self-control, but then I leaned forward and wrapped my arms around his waist, resting my head against his chest. Sam's arms came up slowly and held me close. I could hear his heart, and it seemed to be beating fast. What I wouldn't have given to be held by him just like this all of those years ago. For that one moment I let myself be sixteen and feel all of the warmth and pleasure and comfort from being held by Sam. Then I pushed it away, telling myself it would be the last time I would allow those emotions to rule me.

I pulled away and murmured a good-bye, keeping my eyes on my shoes as I walked out the door and down the sidewalk. I didn't want to look at his face, afraid of what I might see there. Good or bad, it would cause its own kind of pain. I heard the door close quietly behind me. It was the sound of that part of my life ending forever.

Chapter
28

*M*onday and Tuesday rushed by as I shepherded the kids to and from school, helped with homework, kept up the house, and drove us all to the hospital to visit Dad. My own schoolwork continued to slip as I tried to juggle the life of a mother with that of a high school student. Honestly, though, I enjoyed the familiar tasks. It lent a sense of normalcy to an otherwise bizarre situation.

Hannah surprised me. While I took care of the management part of running the household, she became the storyteller, the playmate, and the one the younger kids sat and cuddled with while watching a video. It was a side of her I'd never really seen. She'd always been so standoffish. Both Rachel and Dan really needed her closeness, though Dan would never have admitted it, and it warmed me to see them all piled on the couch while Hannah read Teenage Mutant Ninja Turtles comics aloud.

Sam came over after school both days, and we practiced our piece. I would never pass as a concert pianist, but I figured that most of the time everyone would be so captivated by the amazing sounds Sam would pull from his cello they wouldn't be paying attention to me. He was mostly patient when I messed up the timing or missed a few notes, getting frustrated only when I miscounted the same difficult passage three times in a row.

We had been practicing for two hours when I heard Rachel and Dan arguing in the next room. I knew they were probably hungry. I still needed to make dinner and get to the hospital for a visit, and I just couldn't keep my mind on the music.

"No, Annie," Sam said in exasperation. "It's 'dum da da dum dum

dum.' Count it out. It's a perfect counterpoint for the rhythm I'm playing, but it will be completely lost if you don't get it right."

"I'm sorry. I'm distracted." I played through the phrase again. "Is
that it?"

"Not quite. Here," he said. He rested his cello on its side and came
over to the piano. I watched enviously as his fingers flew fluidly over
the keys, demonstrating the rhythm. "See?" he asked.

"Once more," I said. He played the phrase again, slowing it down
so I could count it out with him. "Okay, I think I've got it." I tried
playing it again and got the rhythm but missed a couple of notes. It
was frustrating.

"It's okay. You'll get it," he said. "Just keep practicing that spot.
The rest is pretty good."

"Thanks, I'll try. Listen, I've got to finish up. I still have a ton of
stuff to do tonight."

"Like what?" he asked as he started packing up his things.

"Dinner, homework, visit my dad, laundry. You know, all that
kind of stuff you accused me of last week." I tried to make it sound like
a joke, but he picked up on the exhaustion in my voice.

"Mom stuff. I get it," he said.

"Yep, that's me. Anyway, I'll try to practice, but it'll probably not
be until tomorrow morning."

"When do you get a chance for music, Annie?" he asked me
abruptly. I was taken aback by the turn of the conversation.

"I told you, tomorrow morning," I said, a little confused.

"No, I mean in the future—what do you do for music? I mean,
you still perform and everything, don't you?" The question seemed to
be really important to him.

"Well, not really. I mean, I did for a while after we got married,
but then things just had to change. When you have a family, things are
different. Priorities start to shift, and what used to be important to you
shifts right along with everything else."

"So you just quit?"

"That's an oversimplification. I didn't quit—not like that," I said. I felt frustrated that he didn't seem to get what I was trying to say. He made it sound like I had given up.

"Well, what else do you call it when you stop doing something that you love? You said that music makes you happy, and you really are talented, especially as a singer. I'm just trying to understand why you'd want to give that up. Why you would even have to."

He was studying me with that look again, that expression that he wore when he was trying to figure me out. I recognized it because I wore that same expression most of the time when we were together. For some reason it just really irritated me now. He had seemed to get it the other night, to understand why I was doing what I was doing. I didn't want him pressing me on the details of my life now. I shouldn't have to defend my choices to him.

"You don't understand. Just wait until you're older and you'll see that life changes, okay? It changes what you want and who you are. When you grow up a bit, you'll understand that."

I got up and started stacking the pages of music and putting them away. Behind me Sam started laughing.

"What?" I asked.

"It's just so funny to hear you talking like my mother," he said. He finished packing up his things, carefully covering his cello strings before closing the case. I started to protest, but he cut me off. "It's not an insult, okay? It's just funny. I'll see you tomorrow."

I closed my mouth, swallowing the argument, and walked with him to the door.

"Yeah, see you tomorrow," I said. I closed the door behind him and went into the kitchen to make dinner.

I tried not to let the matronly comparison sting me. It was true, after all. Still, the last thing I wanted was to have Sam picture me as his mother. I mentally shrugged that thought away. When all was said and done, it really was better this way.

After dinner we went to visit Dad. He was a lot better, able to move around more on his own, and generally feeling more comfortable. Hannah, Rachel, and Dan had been to the hospital only a couple of times, so they still had all the nervousness that went along with the solemn setting. Dad chatted and joked with them, trying to lighten their moods. I laughed along with the others but noticed that Mom was unusually quiet and grave.

"So that's why the food is so nasty here," Dad was saying.

The kids all giggled, Hannah rolling her eyes, and I wondered what the joke had been. Mom let out an exasperated sigh and got up to fuss with Dad's pillows for the third time since we'd arrived. Dad reached out to grasp her hand, and she allowed him to hold it for only a second before pulling away.

"I don't know why they can't seem to bring you water. I guess that's my job, too," she huffed.

She picked up the large plastic mug on the bedside table and left the room. Dad followed her with his eyes, a look of concern on his face, and then he continued to ask Dan about his schoolwork and his plans for the weekend. I excused myself and followed after Mom.

She was standing outside the door in the hall, her arms hanging limply at her sides, the mug dangling from her fingers and just about to fall. She was crying softly, and I felt a shiver of alarm run through me. Had she received some bad news? Maybe Dad wasn't getting better after all.

"Mom, what is it?" I asked, reaching out to take the mug gently from her fingers. At the sound of my voice she quickly wiped away the tears and forced a smile.

"It's nothing, honey, don't worry."

"Is something wrong with Dad, I mean, more wrong?" I asked, my heart in my throat.

"No, no. Nothing like that. He's doing very well, all things considered. It's just—he's always seemed so invincible. I rely on him far too much, and it's just been a shock. I guess I got so caught up in making sure he was going to be okay that I never stopped to consider until now the possibility that he could actually have died."

"But you said yourself that he's going to be fine," I said.

"I know. He is. It's just all hitting me now just how close I came to losing him."

She slid down the wall to sit on the floor. I sat down next to her and wrapped my arms around her, my head resting on her shoulder. The mom that I had become used to in my future never allowed herself to be vulnerable like this. Even though now I was seeing her weakness and fear, she seemed more comforting to me than she had in years, and I longed to soak up that essence, at the same time wanting to comfort her in return. She patted my arm that was across her chest and rested her head on top of mine.

"You know," she said, "I don't deserve your father."

"What? Of course you do. Why would you say something like that?" I asked.

She took a deep breath and let it out in a long exhale.

"He was so confident and personable, so handsome, and I was swept off my feet. I was madly in love with him. I didn't care about the arm—it added to his mystery in some ways. I know it sounds foolish and immature, but when things got hard and money was tight and I was frustrated by him always working and me being stuck home with the kids all day, I started to resent him a little. Not a lot, really, just a little, and every once in a while the idea would pop into my head that I could have married Jeffrey. He made more money, and he had two strong arms." She closed her eyes, and I could see the shame on her face.

"Why didn't you marry Jeffrey?" I asked, suddenly curious about how she had made that decision.

"It just never clicked for me. He asked me to marry him—twice, actually—but I just couldn't say yes. I didn't really understand it at the time myself, but looking back I can see that it would never have worked out. This life, even though it's sometimes hard, is the life that I want, and I wouldn't have had it if I had stayed with Jeffrey. He was an adventurer, but he didn't value the simple things in life. I love being a mom, and I love your father." She turned to look at me. "I really do. I love him, and I couldn't bear to lose him or you kids."

"That's exactly why you deserve Dad, and he deserves you," I said. "You are perfect for each other. He told me about the first time he saw you, just the other day. It's obvious he is still as much in love with you now as he has always been."

Mom smiled and wrapped her arms around me, kissing my forehead.

"When did you grow up?" she asked. "Really, Annie, you have been such a help this last week. I couldn't have handled all of this without you. You're a good girl." She gave me another squeeze and moved to pull away. I grasped her to me all the tighter.

"Mom, promise me that we'll always be close. Please? I don't ever want to grow up and feel like we can't talk like this."

Mom laughed and kept me wrapped in her arms. "Why would that ever happen?" she asked.

"Just promise," I insisted.

"Okay, I promise. But you make me a promise, too, okay? Promise me to always remember that Dad and I love you and that you can talk to us. The street goes both ways, honey."

I nodded against her chest. "I promise."

"Good. Now let's go take care of your dad and maybe take your sisters and brothers down to the cafeteria for pie. What do you think?"

"I think that Dad was a very smart man to marry you, Mom. And pie sounds great." After all, having an actual waistline didn't seem quite so important right now.

Chapter
29

*I*t was after ten when we finally got home. Rachel was asleep in the backseat, and Dan was trying hard not to let his head droop. We pulled into the garage, and he headed straight to his room. I walked Rachel upstairs, helped her take her boots and coat off, and tucked her into bed. The simple act tugged at my heartstrings. I ached for my children.

That ache settled into my chest, and I carried it with me as I went back downstairs to finish the dishes. I was surprised to see Hannah putting the last of them away as I came around the corner.

"Wow, thanks, Hannah. I was just coming down to do those," I said.

She shrugged. "You're not the only one who wants to help Mom," she said. The soft tone she used took the sting out of the words.

"Yeah, I know. Thanks, anyway."

"Sure," she said. She wiped the counters with a towel and hung it on the hook next to the sink to dry. "By the way, we're out of milk. If you want, I can stay here and watch the kids while you go to the store."

I yawned and stretched. Maybe it could wait until the morning. But I knew Dan would explode if he couldn't eat cereal for breakfast.

"You're right. I'd better go before I fall asleep," I sighed. I grabbed my coat and wallet, counting to make sure I had enough money left from what Mom had given me, and then headed to the garage. "I won't be gone long."

A short while later, I loaded the groceries into the backseat of the car, clutching my coat tighter to my body. The wind was picking up, and it looked like we would be having a white Thanksgiving. It was a cold wind, but it was invigorating, too. My earlier exhaustion was gone, and I dreaded going back to the house and trying to sleep.

Even though on the surface it looked like I was keeping things together, I was still having nightmares. Most of them were variations on the one I'd had the week before, where I was trying to catch up with Mitch as he drifted away from me. Sometimes, though, a new element crept in: I was confronted with Mitch on one side and Sam on the other, and whichever way I turned, the other one grew more distant. I wasn't eager to revisit either dream.

I got into the station wagon, started the engine, and let it idle for a few minutes, blowing warm air onto my feet. I scanned through the preset radio stations and came across one of my old favorites. Debbie Gibson's "Lost in Your Eyes." It brought back vivid memories of driving by Sam's house whenever I got a chance to drive the car. I would park down the street a couple of houses away, listen to the radio, and sing along, imagining that I was singing the words to Sam. I rolled my eyes at the memory. Even as I shook my head at my teenage self, I put the car in gear and pulled out of the parking lot. The drive I had decided to make was much longer than the five-minute trip to Sam's house, but it flew by as I sang along to some of those old songs.

I had no plans to go to the door, but the ache in my heart wouldn't ease until I had at least seen Mitch's house tonight. When I got there, the windows were dark except for one light that was on upstairs. It was Mitch's room. As I stared at it, I saw his shadow cross the window. There he was. In that moment I wanted to go to his door so badly that my hands were shaking, but I couldn't figure out how to make the pieces fit properly. Me, a sixteen-year-old, out at eleven o'clock at night, knocking on his door to say . . . what? Instead, I sat motionless in the car and watched the window for a few more minutes until the light finally winked out. I could picture him climbing into bed in his favorite plaid pajama bottoms and a T-shirt.

I started the car again and headed slowly toward the freeway. My heart felt just a little lighter. I had seen his shadow. It was a step. I cherished that memory as I pulled into the garage and unloaded the groceries. I pictured it again and again in my mind as I woke Hannah, who was asleep on the couch, and sent her to bed.

And, as I finally slipped beneath the covers of my own bed, I imagined that he was lying beside me as he had for thirteen years.

"Good night, Mitch," I said, and then I closed my eyes. The nightmares came, but somehow they didn't seem to touch me nearly as much as they had before. It was a step.

Chapter
30

*T*hanksgiving was really getting on my nerves. There was too much laughter as all the cousins ran around like maniacs, yelling and giggling. There was too much chatter as my gaggle of aunts cooked and gossiped in the kitchen, talking at once and answering each other in the middle of their own sentences. There was too much food, carb-laden and greasy, everywhere I looked. I knew I couldn't eat any of it.

Mom saw my frustration and understood. Earlier in the day she had let me know that I would have the house to myself that evening because Hannah, Dan, and Rachel were staying at Aunt Erin's, and Mom was going back to the hospital. Space and time to myself. I saw it for the gift that it was. She caught my eye and winked at me, then nodded. I took it for permission to get out of there, even though dinner wouldn't be ready for a while. I made my excuses to Aunt Erin, hugged and kissed Mom, and then left quickly.

Mom had been driving Dad's sedan, leaving me the station wagon to chauffeur my siblings around. I fished in my jacket pocket for the keys and started the engine, grateful to be escaping. By the time I got home, I was full of anticipation for what I would do with twenty-four hours all to myself.

For the first hour I tried to find something to do. I sifted through my parents' video collection and bookshelves, but nothing even remotely caught my interest. I thought about taking a long bath, but I wasn't really in the mood. Finally, I had to admit defeat. I realized that free time wasn't really what I wanted. Home was what I wanted. This wasn't home.

I had been stuck here for eleven days. Eleven long, long days, and I was homesick. Was I ever going to get home? Did I really, truly have to live this life all over again? I had considered the possibility but had dismissed it. Surely I would get home at some point. Still, if I were here to fix something, to right a wrong, I should have been home by now. Corrie had blown off Jesse. Hannah and I seemed to be doing much better. My parents seemed to understand that I really was trying to change. What more was there to do? Shouldn't I be home now?

I wandered into the kitchen to search for a snack. I hadn't been in the mood to eat at Aunt Erin's, and my stomach was protesting the neglect. Out of the corner of my eye I saw the red light blinking on the answering machine at the end of the counter. I grabbed an apple out of the bowl on the table and pressed the play button while I took a bite. The voice that burst out of the machine brought instant tears to my eyes, and the apple fell from my hand unnoticed.

"Hi, I'm trying to reach an Anne Kelly. I'm not sure if I got the right number, but she stopped by my house last week, and I'm just trying again to reach her. If this is the right number, please have her call me back. My name is Mitch Kelly, and my number is 555-2807." There was a beep, and his voice disappeared. I reached out a trembling hand and pushed the button again to replay the message. He sounded so strong and whole, his deep voice matching his height. I replayed the message over and over, reveling in the sound. I had taken it for granted during our marriage. What a simple thing, to hear the voice of the man that you love day in and day out. Now it was a miracle.

I also realized that I had written the wrong name in the note I gave to Margaret at his house that day. I'd used my married name, Anne Kelly. I'd dropped the "I" in my first name when I went to college. "Anne" had sounded much more professional when I was auditioning. Mitch's message said he would call again. I remembered now that my mom had answered a phone call that she thought was a wrong number when I was sick the week before. Had I been that close and missed him again?

I picked up the phone to call him back, but then hung it up again. What was I going to say? "Hi, I'm Annie May, but I accidentally left the wrong name with you last week"? What would I talk to him about?

This was the same problem I ran into every time I had thought about calling him in the past few days.

"Face it," I told myself out loud. "You are just going to have to wait and meet him when you go to college. You have to be patient if you want things to work out the right way."

I sat at the kitchen counter and replayed the message until the sun went down and the darkness made it hard to see the button. I put my head down on my folded arms. *Face it, Annie,* I thought. *You're pathetic.*

The ringing of the phone startled me, and I quickly answered it, Mitch's voice still running through my mind. The male voice on the other end made my heart race until I realized that it was Sam, not Mitch, calling. Then a different kind of warmth started in my chest.

"I just wanted to see how your Thanksgiving went," he said.

"Pretty lame," I said with a bit of a self-deprecating laugh. "How about yours?"

"Well, Leonard was in rare form. He got drunk and threw the turkey out on the front lawn. My mom got pretty mad, and she and I left and went and had Chinese food. Now he's feeling all sorry, so they are in one of their happy times, cuddling on the couch and watching *It's a Wonderful Life.* It's sickening, actually." He tried to keep his voice light, but I heard the undercurrent of pain that was always there when he spoke of his family.

"Sounds charming," I said.

"So, are you sitting at home, feeling sorry for yourself?" he asked.

"Yep. How about you?"

"The same. Let's go for a drive," he suggested.

I accepted immediately. "Sounds perfect."

"I'll pick you up in five minutes." He hung up. I held the receiver for just a second longer and placed it back on the cradle.

Chapter
31

*L*ess than five minutes later, Sam was there. I opened the door before he could knock.

"Where are we going?" I asked.

"How about pie?"

"Sure. That'll completely blow my diet—sounds wonderful," I joked.

He smiled, and we walked silently to the car. I was a little surprised when he opened the door for me. I hadn't really remembered Sam as a gentleman, but then again, I had been wrong about a lot of things where Sam was concerned.

We drove in comfortable silence to a little diner, and I waited while he opened my door again.

"This is weird," I said. "It's like we're on a date." I was joking, but I could see him deflate a little.

"Aren't we?" he asked.

I searched for something to say, unsure of how to answer, but then he broke into a big grin. "Just kidding. That would be kind of like adultery, right?"

"Ha. Hardly," I laughed. "First of all, I'm not married yet, and second of all, pie wouldn't really count as adultery." Then another thought hit me. "Not to mention that, technically, I'm a widow, so it's okay for me to date."

Our conversation stopped as Sam opened the door to the nearly empty diner. The waitress, an unnatural redhead who appeared to be about seventy, didn't seem happy to see us, but she showed us to a table, handed us menus, and then disappeared into the back.

"I wonder if we'll see her again," I said.

"Be quiet. If you offend her, she'll probably spit in our food."

I laughed and looked over my menu.

"I haven't actually eaten today. I think I'll get some food," I said.

"Good, then I won't feel like a pig. Chinese food never seems to last," he said. He closed his menu and leaned back in his favorite pose with his arms folded across his chest.

The waitress did return and looked only mildly disgruntled at taking our order. While we waited, we chatted about school and music and our families, and I was enjoying myself more than I had in . . . I couldn't even guess how long.

The food was actually quite good, and I ate with relish, enjoying both my meal and the conversation.

"This is really strange, you know," I said as we were nearing the end of our meal.

"What? The fries?" he joked.

"Funny. No—it's just that being here with you is so comfortable. I've had a great time."

"Why is that strange? I thought you liked hanging out with me."

The waitress brought our check, and he pulled out his wallet. I grabbed my purse to get my wallet, but he waved his hand at me.

"It's my treat. Happy Thanksgiving," he said.

"Now it really is like a date," I said.

"That's the second time you mentioned that. Why is it so bad for us to be on a date? I mean, if it's not the adultery thing?"

I stared at him. Hadn't we already covered this?

"Don't panic, Annie. You should see your face," he laughed. "I'm not trying to say that you should give up on your future." He leaned forward and put his hands on the table. "You've made your choice very clear, and I get it. You want Mitch and your kids. Okay, I understand. Here's what I don't get, though: Why haven't you seen him yet?"

"I've tried to see him. It just never works out," I said defensively. I didn't like the turn this conversation was taking.

"No, you haven't."

"Um, yes, I have. You were there. You drove me to his house, remember? I went there again and he still wasn't there, and then I went to his church and he was at our church. I left him a message and he called back, but I missed his call." My excuses were starting to sound thin, even to me, and Sam called me on it.

"Come on, Annie. If you really wanted to see him, you would have. You could have camped out in front of his house until he came out. You could have followed him wherever he went. The way I see it, you know that if you meet him now, you'll be screwing things up."

It was a reflection of my own thoughts, and I had to admit it.

"Yes. I want to see him, but at the same time I'm scared." I picked at the last few fries on my plate. "What if I meet him now and he just thinks I'm a weird teenager, and later, when we normally would have met, he remembers me in a bad way and doesn't want anything to do with me?" I asked. "What if that happens anyway? What if it was just a fluke, him falling in love with me in the first place?" That was the biggest fear of all. I hadn't articulated it before, even to myself. Mitch had seemed like a miracle in my life. What if it was all a mistake? What if it couldn't ever be duplicated?

"Annie," Sam said quietly. His voice was husky. "Why do you do this to yourself? You did it with me, and now you are doing it with him. Why wouldn't someone want to be with you?"

I couldn't help the bitter laugh that broke out of my throat.

"Seriously? Let me list the reasons," I said, ticking them off on my fingers as I spoke. "I'm fat—I'm working on it, but I still have a good twenty-five pounds to lose. I'm mediocre at everything I do. I want to be a musician, but I'm really not good enough to be professional. I'm emotionally a mess half the time, and I end up dragging others into it with me. What other reason do you need?"

Sam's lips pressed into a hard line, and he leaned forward with a furious look in his eyes.

"I don't ever want to hear you talk about yourself like that again. Ever. How can you say stuff like that?"

"Because it's the truth. I've never been delusional about my talent or my looks, but at least I thought I was a good person. Revisiting my life like this has awakened me to the fact that I'm not the wholesome, giving person that I thought I was."

Sam stood up abruptly, leaving the money on the table, and gestured to the door.

"Come on. I want to show you something." His expression was serious, and I wondered where he was taking me, but I stood, put on my jacket, and followed him out the door.

We drove in silence for about fifteen minutes, heading for a part of town that I hadn't ever really seen before. It was an industrial area without any houses or storefronts, and I wondered what he could possibly want to show me here. He finally pulled up to a deserted spot on the side of the road. The businesses faced away from the road here, and it was a lonely, solitary place. Off to the right was a jumble of train tracks leading in different directions. We must have been near the train station, but I hadn't recognized it from the direction that we had traveled.

Sam put the car in park and let the engine idle.

"What is this place?" I asked. What could he possibly want to show me here? There didn't seem to be anything of interest in sight.

"This is where we were when my mom told me that my dad wasn't coming home. I was ten, and my dad and I were really close. You know that story already. Anyway, I used to ride my bike over here when I was younger." I thought about the distance. That was some bike ride.

"That must have been really hard."

"Yeah. Well, that was the easy part. My dad was gone, but things got better with my mom for a long time. When she met Leonard, she was really happy at first. It was a few months after they got married before all the bad stuff started. The first time he beat her up, I came here. I had to get out of the house, and I had nowhere else to go. I was fascinated with the trains that run through here. I used to put pennies on the tracks or bottle caps or pop cans, just to see what the trains would do to them." He stared out the window for a minute, and I could see the younger version of Sam in his place. It was a lonely thought.

"Eventually I started to wonder what the trains would do to *me* if I was the one on the tracks." He ignored my sharp breath and continued. "I wasn't serious about it or anything. It was just morbid curiosity, until one weekend. You know how Leonard always gets drunk on weekends and holidays? Well, he's drunk half the time at church, too. This was about three years ago. It was Sunday morning, and he was determined that we all should go to church even though he was still plastered. I refused to go, and my mom stood up to him. She didn't want to be seen in church with him like that. He didn't even bother trying to hide it. He shoved us out the door to the car. My mom didn't even have her shoes on, and he hit her in the mouth when she tried to argue. I was arguing with him up until that point, but I stopped, knowing it would only make things worse for my mom.

"So we went to church. We sat in the back row, and my mom was trying to hide her swollen mouth and her bare feet. It was the worst thing I could think of, Leonard sitting there all holier-than-thou with his wife barefoot and her mouth still bleeding into her tissue. As we were leaving, we passed you and your father. He stood up and shook my mother's hand and told her that he was happy we had made it today. He promised her that he'd be checking in on her later to see how the family was doing, and then he glared at Leonard with an awful expression on his face. It was awesome. I think Leonard was scared enough to wet his pants with that look your dad gave him.

"And you. You were wearing this blue dress that your mom made, and you smiled at me and told me that the music had been really pretty. It wasn't anything big at the time, and I didn't think much of it, other than being grateful that at least some people in this town were looking out for my mom.

"When we got home and he passed out, I told my mom that nothing was worth this garbage and we needed to get out of there. And do you know what she did? She defended him. She said he was right and that there was no excuse for us not to be in the Lord's house on His day. She wouldn't even let me talk to the bishop." He gritted his teeth and smacked the steering wheel hard with his fist. He breathed hard for a minute, and I watched as the memory replayed, all the pain and helplessness of the situation flickering across his face. Finally he continued.

"That night I walked here and stared at the trains for a long time. I thought about doing it for real then. I could see a train coming that way." He pointed to the left. "I knew that it would be quick and I wouldn't have to deal with his garbage anymore. I wouldn't have to watch my mom beat up and humiliated anymore. It was close. Only two things stopped me. One was that I just couldn't leave my mom alone to face him by herself—and the other was you. You and your dad caring about us. You in that blue dress. You stood by your father while he threatened Leonard, and you smiled. You trusted him completely, and that made me want to believe him, too. It made me wonder what it must be like to live in the world that you lived in. Your smile made it seem like life really didn't have to be all bad."

I swallowed hard at all that he had said and implied. Sam's life really was so much more complicated than I had understood. His complaints about Leonard to me had really never been much more than that. There had been no details shared, just vague allusions to the fact that he was a drunk and abusive. The loneliness and helplessness he must have felt hurt me to think of it, and the thought of him contemplating suicide was abhorrent. It took a few minutes for me to find my voice.

"I remember that day," I finally said. "I was fairly clueless to what was going on. I knew my dad was trying to help in some way, but I didn't get it. The thing I remember most is that you hardly looked at me. See, that's what I mean. I was too wrapped up in worrying about whether you were noticing me to actually pay attention to what you were going through."

"I'm *glad* you didn't get it. You were just a kid. The point was that you were there. Everyone else at church, and in this town, for that matter, has always turned a blind eye or a critical one. They don't care about my mom or about me, just about the fact that we don't fit in. That *I* don't fit in is more like it. You've never treated me that way. You've always have made me feel welcome. Like I actually matter. You don't know what that means to me. You have friends and family, but I have never had anyone but you."

I had to fight away the warmth of being so close to him. It was making it hard for me to find the right words. "Sam, you are *not* alone, and you really don't see yourself very clearly. Bishop Michaels, Mr. Allan—they care about you, too. Not to mention that you always have girls hanging around waiting for your attention and the guys all want to be your friends. You always have had that kind of aura about you that makes people think you have a secret that they wish they knew. You are dynamic, and people want to be around you."

He laughed at that description. "What a joke. The only secret I usually have is that my life is awful, and I'm trying to act like it isn't."

I'd never seen him be this open about his family. He always tried to act like he was tough and could handle it all. The wall had cracked a little, and I was getting a glimpse of the man inside.

"What I'm trying to say, Annie, is that you talk about yourself like that, and it hurts me. You've saved my life more than once. You've kept me wondering what crazy thing you were going to do or say next, and it's made me want to keep going. I didn't realize that I felt more than that until you started talking about Mitch. Maybe I never would have—that seems to be what you've told me has happened before . . . or in the future, or whatever—but that seems really hard to believe. My world revolved around you, and I didn't even know it. Now that I know it, I don't know how to just stop feeling that way."

He turned to me, and I found myself leaning toward him. His eyes were dark with that same burning intensity that usually sent shivers down my spine. This time it was more than that, though. That look lit a fire inside me. I knew he was going to kiss me, and this time I didn't pull away. I closed my eyes.

Whenever I'd imagined kissing Sam—which I'd done about a million times—I had pictured something passionate and desperate, probably because that was how I felt. This, however, was a slow, hot, smoldering kiss.

He brushed his lips across mine gently, his hands coming up to cup my head. I mirrored his movements, burying my fingers in the hair that curled slightly at the back of his neck.

He pulled back and stared at me, his eyes taking in my parted lips and wide eyes. "Annie, I love you."

He clutched me to him, his lips seeking mine again. My heart felt like it would explode with joy. How many years had I longed for this moment? How many nights had I lain awake in my room, creating just such an image in my mind? I had been very creative, letting my imagination run wild, wondering just what it would be like to have Sam love me. The most amazing thing was that the reality was even better than I had imagined. The intensity that always was there in Sam's eyes was there in his kiss and in his words. I felt loved, cherished. In that moment I was blissful.

Mostly.

I shoved that thought away. There was no reason that I couldn't love Sam, be with him now, have a relationship that lasted for the next few years until it was time for Mitch. Even Mitch's name couldn't drag me away from Sam's kiss. His hands were buried in my hair, and I groaned in the joy of being loved. I continued to kiss him back, allowing my vivid imagination to create a vision of a future spent, at least for a while, with Sam. He would understand. He knew what was at stake. Surely he wouldn't ask me to give up my family. Then maybe we could find each other again in the future. It was possible. That thought allowed me to continue. Then thought was replaced simply with the pleasure of Sam's kisses.

I don't know how much time passed, only that eventually thought began to return. At first it was the same image of being with Sam for as long as possible, and then it shifted to the moment that it would end. I would have to tell him that it was over. Sam wasn't the kind of guy to just get bored and wander away. To him, commitment meant commitment. I would have to be the one to end it. The look of pain on his face when we discussed Leonard's treatment of his mother flashed into my head. That was the look of someone whose heart was breaking. How could I ever willfully be the one to cause that look to reappear?

But wouldn't it be the same now? He loved me. What would it do to him now if I chose Mitch over him? Maybe I had already experienced that life, and now it was time for a different one. That thought scared me back to reality, and I broke away with a gasp.

"What is it?" he asked. His face was so beautiful. I couldn't look at him and say what I had to say. I pulled away and backed toward the door. "Annie?" he asked in alarm.

"Why?" I asked, my voice cracking. "Why does everything have to be so hard? Why, Sam? Why couldn't you have loved me then? When I didn't already know what my life was supposed to be? If that had happened I would never have had to miss Mitch. I never wanted anything else but you until then. So why now? Now, when everything that I love is at stake? I just don't understand!" I shouted those last words and punched at the dashboard. The tears started again, but I didn't care. Sam stared at me, unblinking.

"Why did God send me back? What was the point of all of this? Am I supposed to change my future? Give up my children? What? What am I supposed to do?" I was so furious, so helpless, that I couldn't contain it. I was yelling now.

"I didn't want to love you again, but I do. I love you and I love him and I love my kids, and none of these things can go together—don't you see that?" My voice broke. Buried thoughts were boiling to the surface.

"If it was just between Mitch and you, then I don't know what I would do. I love him so much, but he died. Maybe it would be better not to have to go through that again. What am I saying? I'd give *anything* not to have to go through that again. But it happened. He died, and there was nothing that could be done, nothing that could be changed. Sure, a little more exercise might have postponed it, but eventually he would have died anyway. The aneurysm was in a part of his brain that they couldn't reach, so nothing that I can do is going to prevent it from happening again. I could just let that go and be with you. Maybe I could."

There was hope flaring in Sam's eyes, and I knew I had to stamp it out before it burned us both. "But my kids. Mallory and Jenna and James. They are my children. Do you know what that means? My *children*, Sam. I can't ever, ever let that go. I can't just pretend that they don't matter. Dealing with Mitch's death was the most horrible thing I've ever gone through, but I would do it ten times over if I had to, for them."

I dropped my head in my hands.

"So why am I here? Did I screw everything up so much that I have to relive it again just to make sure I suffer enough? And what about you? The first time around you didn't regret me. Now you are wrapped up in this. Now you love me, too, just like I loved you—still do. Yes, I still love you. But what can I do, Sam? I have to let you go. I have to because holding on will only hurt you more."

"Maybe you should let me make that decision. I've been thinking about this since last week, and I have a plan. I get what you are saying about your kids. I wouldn't take that away from you. We'll be together until Mitch, and then I'll wait for you. Twenty years isn't that long." He tried to smile, but it fell flat, and he gave up the attempt. "We can still have time together."

His words so closely matched my earlier thoughts that I was

swayed for a millisecond, but that image of his face racked with pain wouldn't leave me.

"No, Sam, we can't. You don't deserve that, and I don't know how to love two people at the same time. I'm already going crazy. What would it be like in three years when we're even more in love? That's what love is like, you know. It gets stronger, not the other way around. How could I leave you then? I would be too tempted to stay. Besides, what if something happened to mess everything up? What if I got pregnant?" He started, and his eyes shot to my face. "It could happen, and you know it. But it's not just that. There are so many things that could go wrong. Then I would end up hating you for it, your fault or not, and you don't deserve that.

"As for waiting for me, that's just crazy. You have so much to give. You need to find someone else to love."

I couldn't keep the pain out of my voice at that thought. Sam heard it and shook his head.

"No. There isn't anyone else."

"Miranda . . ." I started, but he cut me off.

"She's really not my type."

"You liked her well enough before, believe me. But it doesn't have to be her. Who knows who you might meet at college? You can get your scholarship and go to school and have a lot of success. You'll meet someone, and you'll be happy."

"I don't like you playing matchmaker for me," he gritted out.

I slumped against the seat. "I know. I'm sorry. It's all so stupid. All I'm saying is that this can't work. I love you, Sam. Part of me has always loved you, but I can't be with you."

That hurt so badly that I couldn't continue speaking. Sam was quiet for a moment, staring out the windshield, and then he quietly nodded. His acquiescence was a relief and a blow. That nod saved me, and I knew it. If he had pressed me much more I might have given in, and I would have regretted it forever. I was so grateful and yet so heartbroken.

A whimper broke through, and Sam turned, catching my expression. He groaned and wrapped his arms around me again, this time in a comforting embrace. I cried quietly for a few minutes as he held me and rubbed my back. Finally the tears dissipated, and I pulled away.

"Time to get home," he said quietly.

I nodded, exhausted.

Sam held my hand as he drove. We were both quiet. There wasn't anything left to cover. The cold night was settling into my bones, and I was shivering by the time we reached my house. I was grateful not to have to explain my late night to anyone. He pulled into the driveway, and we sat together for just a few minutes more. I knew that when I exited this car I would be leaving him behind forever. No matter how much we might see each other after this at school or church, things could never be the same again. I knew that, even though I hated it. I couldn't remain his friend without us both wanting more. There was too much between us, too much chemistry, or whatever else it may have been.

My hand was warm in Sam's. I wrapped my fingers tightly around his and looked at him.

"Thank you, Sam. For everything." I hoped my eyes said the rest. *Thanks for being there for me. Thanks for understanding me. Thanks for loving me.* I could see the answer in his face. It echoed my thoughts.

He brought my hand to his lips and kissed my fingers, one by one.

"Goodnight, Annie." *Good-bye,* his eyes said. My eyes filled with tears again, and I tried to blink them back. Impulsively, I leaned forward and kissed him one last time, and then I opened the car door and bolted through the frigid night into my house.

I closed the door behind me and leaned against it, sliding down in a heap on the floor as I listened for the sound of his car. He sat there for a few minutes before finally backing away. Then I heard him accelerate too fast down the street. Would he go home or back to the tracks?

I climbed slowly up the stairs and got into bed fully clothed. I let myself cry for the last time over Sam. It took a long time for the tears to be gone.

Chapter
33

Dad came home on Sunday, and it was like an early Christmas. The trip home made him tired, but he still smiled beautifully at the "Welcome home" signs that we had all made for him. He hugged each one of us before making his way slowly up the stairs with Mom on one side and me on the other. By the time we got him settled he was exhausted, but he sighed with satisfaction at being home in his own bed before he fell asleep.

I was so glad to have him home. I had never quite recovered from my talk, or argument, or breakup, or whatever it was with Sam on Thanksgiving, and I had spent far too much time alone thinking about it and replaying every little nuance in his expression, every word that either of us had spoken. I was just as sad to have broken his heart—broken mine in the process, too—as I had been that night, but I had found a measure of comfort in knowing that I had made the right choice. That comfort was small, though, knowing that I would be seeing him at the concert the next day. I'd been worrying about it since I woke up, and I was grateful for the distraction of helping Mom to take care of Dad.

Dad was too perceptive nowadays, though. When I checked on him later in the afternoon, he was awake and hungry. I brought him up some low-fat, low-sodium soup, which he grimaced at but ate dutifully. While he ate he studied my face. I tried to make small talk about the things that had happened while he was gone, but I was not doing a very good job.

"You've been worrying again, haven't you, baby cakes?" Dad asked.

"Just about the concert tomorrow night. The sonata that Sam and

I are playing is really difficult. I keep worrying that I'll mess it up and ruin his chance for a scholarship," I said. I managed to keep my voice even when I said his name. I was only partially lying. I really was worried about the scholarship for Sam. It's just that I was worrying about a lot more than that, too.

"I'm sure you'll do just fine, Annie," Dad said. It startled me a little that he didn't call me by my nickname, and I looked at his face more closely. His eyes were filled with compassion and interest. It struck me then just how blessed I was to have such wonderful parents. Even though Mom and I fought sometimes and didn't get along much when I got older, I never had to doubt that they would be there if I really needed them. Since I had been home I felt closer than ever to both my parents, but to Dad especially.

"Dad, can I ask you something?"

"Sure. What's up?"

"Do you remember a few years back when Brother Sharp came to church drunk and Sister Sharp wasn't wearing any shoes?"

"That's a strange thing to remember. I didn't even know you'd noticed what was going on. What brought that up?"

"I was just thinking about it the other day. I don't remember what you said, but I think you kind of threatened him or something. Why was that?" Dad gave me a small smile, and there was a twinkle in his eye.

"Some people are bullies. Usually they're just afraid, and they take it out on people who are weaker than themselves. In my experience, the best way to deal with a bully is to make sure he knows that what he does is not going unobserved. I don't remember threatening him, but he might have taken it that way. That was fine by me." I smiled at the description. It was true—people listened to my dad and respected him.

"So you just implied that he would be in big trouble if he hurt her again and left it at that?"

"Well—not exactly." He seemed to be embarrassed for some reason.

"What else?"

"I figured that with Leonard it wouldn't be enough to just imply. He was probably drunk enough that he'd talk himself out of the whole thing as soon as he sobered up and be right back to his old behaviors. So, every once in a while I check in on them. I look for excuses to stop by—a message from the bishop or a delivery of some of your mom's homemade bread. Little things, just so he knows that I'm still watching. I don't know if it's made a difference or not." He shrugged and waved his hand.

"Are you blushing, Dad?" I laughed.

"Are you kidding?" he said. He smiled again. "What brought this up, anyway? That was years ago."

"I was talking to Sam the other day, and he mentioned it. It really meant a lot to him that you would stand up for him and his mom. He still remembers it. I think it *has* made a difference."

"Wow, I didn't even remember that he was in earshot of the whole thing." The subject obviously made Dad uncomfortable. He always taught us to do good but to try to do it quietly, anonymously if possible, and recognition was definitely not the goal. I dropped the subject, making just one last comment.

"Thanks for doing that, Dad. It means a lot to me too." I gave him a hug, kissing his cheek, and then walked toward the door.

"Annie Bell, you'll do great tomorrow. You just remember that you are not alone. I'll be listening from here." Dad smiled at me, and I felt encouraged. His warm smile lodged somewhere in my chest, and I knew that I could make it through.

I needed that smile with me as I faced school the next day. Everyone involved in the music program was nervous and wired. We were excused from our morning classes to set up the stage and put the last-minute preparations on our program. The Winterfest was the kickoff for the Christmas season, not just for the school but for much of the town, and we put a lot of work into it. We prepared Christmas music as well as a sampling of the types of pieces that the students had worked on through the first half of the year.

I was participating in seven numbers in addition to the sonata, three with the orchestra and four with the a cappella choir. For me it meant three different outfits and very precise timing to make it from each set to the next. Usually this was the type of thing I craved. Performing was invigorating to me, and the day of a performance usually found me as energized as the rest of my classmates.

Not today.

Today was an ending. I discovered just how stark an ending it was going to be when Sam and I did our last run-through during first period. We were in one of the practice rooms off the orchestra room, a tiny little place with a spinet piano and a chair and little space for anything else. We were crammed in tightly, and it was awkward as we carefully avoided bumping each other. There was a restraint in our conversation that hailed back to a couple of years before when we hadn't known each other very well. We were each trying to make it easier for the other, and we were both failing.

"You've got to get that downbeat," Sam blurted after I missed the opening cadence for the third time in a row. He counted it out, slapping his leg in time with the rhythm.

"I know, Sam. I'm not an idiot," I snapped. "I just can't seem to get it. I can hear it in my head, but I just can't seem to make my fingers get there in time. I'm doing the best I can, okay?" I was instantly sorry. It wasn't his fault that I was so much slower than he was.

"I'm sorry," he said, sweeping a hand through his hair. "Just try a one, three, four fingering instead, and it might help." His tone was much softer. "Sorry I snapped."

"Yeah, me, too. It's my fault anyway. Let's try it again." He nodded, and we went through it a couple more times. His tip about the fingering helped, and I didn't miss my entrance again.

"You've got it," he said finally.

"Thanks. You sound great, of course. I'm sure that this will be a huge step toward that scholarship," I said.

"I'm not going for the scholarship. I'm going to my dad's." My heart plummeted to my shoes.

"When? Why?" I asked. I already knew the answer to the second question, though.

He smiled sadly, acknowledging the same thought. "Tomorrow, actually. In the morning." He laid his cello carefully on its side and crouched down, packing up his things.

"Why the rush?" My voice sounded hollow.

"Come on, Annie, you know why. I just can't do this. It'll be better to get away from Leonard, anyway, and spend some time with my dad. It's been years, after all." He looked up. "There's nothing more to keep me here."

I replayed that moment again and again as I helped to set up risers and sorted through my music, making sure everything was in order. There had been just the hint of challenge in his eyes. Give me a reason to stay, they had said. He knew I couldn't, but he was like me, desperate for a better way to get through this.

But there was no better way. This was the only way, and it was probably best that he go to his dad's. He'd done it the first time around, after all. Only this time I wouldn't be writing to him, interfering with his girlfriend. That thought blistered through my mind, and I slammed my binder of music down a little too forcefully on the piano lid.

"Mallory. Jenna. James," I muttered under my breath. They were the reason I was doing this. I just had to hold tight to them in my mind, and I would get through this. "Mitch," I added, even more quietly. It hurt to know that I had been feeling more distant from him with all of the upheaval about Sam. Mitch, too. He was also the reason.

Their names were a silent chant in my head for the rest of the day. My last day seeing Sam. Every time we passed in the hall or backstage, moving things around, I knew it was one of the last moments I would see him. Time seemed to play tricks on me, leaping forward every time our paths crossed, so that it sped by in lightning-like flashes, and then slowing down to a snail's pace when he wasn't around.

At least I hadn't had to go to therapy today. With Dad's illness I'd managed to get out of it the week before, but Mom had been adamant that I not miss two weeks in a row. I had Dad's interference to thank for my reprieve. Mom's look of shock when he had bellowed, "Mary, enough! She's not going today!" had been hilarious. Even funnier was the fact that she actually seemed to have liked his forcefulness.

The bell signaling the end of the school day brought my head up in a disoriented panic.

"What was that?" I asked.

"Relax, Annie, it's just the last bell," Corrie said. She'd been eyeing me strangely all day, and I finally decided I had to tell her something at least.

"Sam is moving to California to live with his dad in the morning," I blurted.

Her mouth formed a little round "o," and her eyes went wide. "Wow, that . . . that really stinks," she said. It was so straightforward. The perfect description.

"Yeah. Totally," I said, sounding exactly like my original sixteen-year-old self. From that moment on, she became overly sympathetic, eyeing me with compassion that bordered on the melodramatic.

Before I knew it we were changing into our dresses for A Cappella and lining up outside the door to the stage. I could hear the hum of the audience as the families of the students and other members of the community rushed in to find their seats. Normally I would have been feeling the exhilaration of adrenaline pumping through my veins. Instead I only felt vaguely dizzy and a little nauseated.

"Are you okay?" Samantha, the alto next to me in line, asked. "You look a little green."

"I think so," I said. She looked like she was going to question me further, but the noise from the crowd died down, and we heard Miss Lund announcing us. The choir filed out, we took our place on the risers, and the performance began.

Chapter

34

The first chords of "Adeste Fideles," in tight a cappella harmony, rang out across the now silent audience. The thrill of performing suddenly hit me, and I breathed it in with relief. The craziness of the day dissipated, and the overdue surge of adrenaline flooded my bloodstream, energizing me and bringing the room into sharp focus. I felt the tingle of it down to my fingertips. My voice, faltering at first, now joined confidently with the others as we sang the classic Christmas hymn.

Memories flooded over me—memories of my children rushing downstairs on Christmas morning, Mitch and me cuddled together in front of a fire in our tiny apartment on our first Christmas morning. They were poignant and sweet memories. I could almost taste them. They buoyed me up and gave me extra confidence. The harmonies of the music seemed even closer, more thrilling, when they accompanied the pictures in my mind.

We sang three more songs—two carols and a classic madrigal— and then the race was on. The jazz band was performing a couple of crowd-pleasers, and I had about ten minutes to change my clothes, get my other music folder, and be on the other side of the stage to line up with the orchestra. I rushed past Sam and a couple of the other guys. They had it easy. A tux was a tux, after all.

Corrie followed behind me as we made a beeline for the dressing room. She unzipped my dress and grabbed my skirt and blouse while I quickly pulled my hair back into a large barrette.

"Don't forget your shoes," she called out as I nearly left the room in just my stockings.

"Thanks," I said breathlessly as I grabbed the shoes. I ran around the back hall and made it just in time to hurriedly slip them on and then walk out sedately with the rest of the group. Sam was behind me, and he chuckled at the change in my gait. I couldn't help grinning in response.

As luck, or Mr. Allan, would have it, the piano parts for all of our orchestra songs were fairly sedate. Maybe he just had mercy on my overburdened repertoire, or maybe something was finally going to go my way. Whatever the reason, I made it through the numbers without any glaring mistakes.

Our last piece ended, and the audience applauded as first Mr. Allan and then the entire orchestra stood and bowed. My heart was already racing in anticipation of the hardest part of the evening.

It was tradition that the soloists would dress in formal attire. For Sam and the other male performers that was easy. They were already wearing those tuxedos. But for all of the female performers it meant yet another costume change. I walked offstage as quickly as the slowly filing orchestra line would allow, kicked off my shoes, and ran to the other side of the stage, back to the dressing room. Corrie was waiting for me with my performance gown.

It was a dress that I had worn last year to my cousin Elisa's wedding. Deep teal with a tightly fitted bodice, it flared out to the floor in rippling waves. It was beautiful, perfect for this kind of performance, with short sleeves that wouldn't impede my hands as I played. The shoes didn't really match, and I hoped that no one would pay too much attention to them. But all in all I felt quite pretty in the dress, or at least I would have if I'd had time to look at myself in the mirror before running back out to wait in the wings once again for our turn.

Sam was waiting for me. His cello would be placed on the stage by Mr. Allan. It was the first time I had a chance to really look at him. He was striking in his tuxedo, looking like he owned it, as opposed to the awkward way that most of the students wore theirs.

He smiled at me as I came to join him. The number before us, a horn quartet, was still playing, and I breathed deeply, grateful for the chance to really catch my breath.

"Nervous?" he asked softly.

"Of course. You?"

"Never," he said with a grin.

I smiled back at him warmly, so grateful for his friendship.

"Good luck, Sam," a female voice said from behind us. We both turned, and I grimaced at the sight of Miranda in all of her redheaded, overly made-up glory. She came forward and made a show of straightening Sam's tie unnecessarily. I fought the urge to slap her hands away.

"Thanks," Sam said, without feeling.

"Not that *you'll* need it," she continued, now brushing his shoulders. Her gesture was ridiculously intimate, and her message was clear. *He* wouldn't need the luck, but I would. I turned away from her and grabbed Sam's hand.

"It's our turn," I said as the brass quartet finished to a healthy applause. I pulled him forward, ignoring Miranda's caustic comment behind me.

Just before we walked onto the stage, I moved to free my hand, but Sam clutched it just a moment longer, squeezing my fingers to reassure me.

"You'll be great. Just remember—one, three, four. Right?"

I nodded, and he released my hand. Mr. Allan introduced us, and I could hear my sisters and Mom cheering for me in the far left section of the auditorium. We walked to center stage where the grand piano and a chair, music stand, and Sam's cello were waiting for us.

All of my nervousness returned full force as we both took our places. My fingers were tingling, and I silently prayed that I wouldn't make any obvious mistakes that would detract from the beauty of Sam's performance. I took a deep breath and placed my fingers on the keys.

"One, three, four," I whispered silently and began the introduction. I even remembered Sam's rhythm instructions and managed to make it through the sticky part. Sam joined me, the warm tones of his cello somehow light and flowing like waves on the beach or slow, deep breaths just before falling asleep, then forceful when it was called for. I forgot myself and just let my fingers follow his lead.

The movement that we were playing was six minutes long, and each minute arrived, grew, and departed in equal measure, the music filling every space within the time. Even as I was in the middle of it, I knew that this high school auditorium had never hosted any performance of this caliber and probably never would again. It was technically perfect, on Sam's part anyway, and I at least managed to cover all my mistakes so that they would be obvious only to someone who was intimately familiar with the piece.

My favorite part arrived. It was a passage where I just played strong chords as Sam wove intricately flowing arpeggios that dazzled the ear and created amazing tension. Finally, the resolution. A breathtaking series of descending scales that finished with a flourish in true Schubert style. It was over.

The crowd burst into an appreciative applause. I rose and curtsied next to Sam. The crowd applauded me, but when Sam bowed they went wild. Even these small-town families and high school students knew that they were hearing something truly remarkable. I glanced to the side to see Sam's reaction. He was breathing heavily, and I could see that he was deeply moved by the respect the audience held for him as an artist. He smiled and reached for my hand, then raised it slightly, and we bowed together again.

I turned to walk from the stage, but he released my hand and didn't follow. I glanced at him in surprise.

"I have another number," he whispered as he turned to the piano. I nodded and walked off the stage, bemused. The program didn't say anything about another number between our sonata and the finale.

I stood in the wings and watched, wondering what Sam would play. He didn't have any sheet music with him, and I got a premonition, a memory really, as he gently placed his hands on the keys and began to play.

It began as a simple melody, written in a major key but with surprising chording, and then it evolved. The melody was joined by a chasing harmony played in counterpoint that wrapped around, under, and through the melody, changing it to something much deeper. Sam was playing my song. The one that he had originally written for his mother, now written for me. How had I forgotten about this? I guess somehow some things hadn't changed, or at least they hadn't disappeared. I was moved to tears to think that I could have inspired something so strong and passionate in him. I didn't deserve it. I was sure of that.

The rest of the choir was gathering together and lining up behind me, preparing for our entrance when Sam finished playing. They jostled and whispered and joked in their excitement. I tried to ignore them and focus on the music. This was the most profoundly humbling experience I had ever had next to the moments when each of my children had been placed in my arms for the first time. It was beauty and creation. It was love and acceptance and desire.

And it was also good-bye. I could feel that through every chord, every measure, every beat. The message was clear.

He finished the last three measures, ending in a sudden minor key shift that left a melancholy longing in the air. The audience was silent for just a moment, then erupted in applause. Again the remarkable had been presented to them, this time far more raw and emotion-driven than our technical piece ever could have been. They didn't know that they had just witnessed Sam's soul being poured out in front of them.

I didn't clap along with the rest. Such a raucous response just didn't seem appropriate after something so intimate, so vulnerable.

"Let's go, Annie," Samantha said, and I realized that the various musicians, choir, orchestra, and jazz band were all filing past me to fill the stage for our final number.

I allowed myself to be swept along with them, only half aware of my surroundings. The song was still playing in my head, and I could see only Sam. The rest of the room seemed to have faded around him, the color leached out somehow.

He wasn't looking at me. We were all jumbled together, with no structured formation, as we sang "We Wish You a Merry Christmas." People were singing arm in arm, and I noticed that Miranda had managed to worm her way through the crowd to Sam's side. Her arm draped around his waist. His own arm hung awkwardly.

Then it was over. The audience cheered and rose to their feet, clapping and calling out the names of their sons and daughters and friends. I tried to look at them, to acknowledge the applause with a smile or a bow like the other students, but I could only stare at Sam.

We were separated by at least a dozen people, but I saw him quite clearly as he caught my eye, then turned toward the audience and nodded his head, gesturing to somewhere in the crowd. I followed his gaze, and my heart quit beating.

It was Mitch.

Chapter
35

He stood next to Margaret, clapping along with the rest of the crowd, just another member of the community coming to the concert as a kickoff to the Christmas season.

"Mitch," I whispered, but the sound was lost in the uproar. He was there, alive. Beautifully, vibrantly alive and right in front of me. All the noise in the room, the mayhem of students rushing off the stage to greet their families and be congratulated for the performance, just disappeared. There was only Mitch and me.

But wait—wasn't there supposed to be someone else, too? Sam.

I glanced back at him. He was watching me, just as unaware of the chaos surrounding us as I was, and his heart was in his eyes, for all to see if they had known to look.

"I love you," he said. I couldn't hear his voice from where I was but the words were clear just the same.

"Wait, Sam!" I called out, and I started toward him.

Samantha was in my way, and she seemed to move in the same direction as I did every time I tried to step around her. Finally I pushed past her, but Sam had headed toward the stairs. "Wait!" I called again.

He turned back to me and shook his head, then pointed back to Mitch, who was helping Margaret with her coat. They were leaving. I was grounded to the spot.

This was the moment. The decision that I had thought had come and gone already. It was time to make my choice. Sam was leaving, moving away to be with his dad, and I would have to let him go if I chose Mitch. He would walk out of the auditorium and out of the school, and I would never see him again.

Mitch was here, at least for now. He was also leaving. Who knew if our future was assured? Was it worth giving up Sam to have another chance with Mitch, however brief it might be?

It was then that I saw Mitch catch sight of Sam. He raised a hand and waved at him. Sam nodded and waved back, and an amazing thought popped into my head. Sam had met Mitch at the church. Had he invited him here tonight?

Miranda appeared at Sam's side and grabbed his hand, tugging at it to try to get his attention. He continued to stare at me. I knew then, to the depth of my bones, just how much I was giving up.

"Good-bye. I love you. Thank you," I said quietly. Just as I had heard his words earlier, I could see that he heard mine, however softly they might have been spoken. He blinked once, then he turned and walked off the stage.

I watched him for a moment, and then reality hit me. I twisted around to look back at the place where Mitch had been. He was gone. I searched the room frantically, heading toward the stairs on the other side of the stage. There he was. He and Margaret were already halfway out of the room, mostly lost in the crowd.

"Mitch!" I called out, but it wasn't loud enough for him to hear me. I rushed down the stairs and up the aisle, trying to push past the people blocking my way.

"Slow down, Annie!" my mom called from behind me.

I had forgotten she was even there. I ignored her and kept pushing through the people. I caught sight of Margaret's plaid coat as she and Mitch left the auditorium and made it into the foyer that led to the doors outside. I was breathing heavily with effort and emotion. It felt like I was moving through thick sand up to my hips. "Please, wait," I panted, and the tears wouldn't be held back anymore. I was going to miss him again. I just needed to talk to him, just for a moment. It would be enough to carry me through for now, but even that was being denied me.

An irritable man, the father of one of the band kids, glared at me as I tried to squeeze between him and his son. "Watch out," he grumbled.

"I'm sorry," I mumbled. I pushed through anyway, but I had lost sight of Mitch and Margaret. Had they already left?

A couple of kids were horsing around and laughing, and they bumped into the same man. He turned to glare at them, and his foot came down on my dress just as I stepped forward. He stumbled, my movement pulling him off balance, and he backed up to catch himself, knocking me over. I fell, and the hem of my dress ripped.

I landed on my hands and knees, and the defeat was bitter in my mouth. Once again I had missed my chance, only this time I had hurt Sam in the process and torn out half of my heart as well. I wanted to stay right there on that floor. Just stay there, hidden by the crowds of people, the noise drowning out any thought. Maybe I could just melt into the ugly high school carpet and disappear forever.

"Are you okay?" The voice was quiet, but every other noise in the crowded foyer disappeared from my hearing. I looked up slowly. Could it possibly be, after all this time?

There he was, leaning over me, his broad shoulders creating a sheltered space in the crowd and his blue eyes filled with concern. "Are you hurt? Can I help you up?" He reached out a hand to steady me, and I took it. A thrill shot up my arm at the contact with him, and I drew a long breath. Sweet, cool air filled my lungs with strength and calm that spread through my whole body. This was my home.

"Thank you," I managed to squeak, and my eyes locked onto his.

"Sure. It's quite the crowd. I've never been to this concert before. I'm surprised at how many people are here. Not that it wasn't great. It was. Great, that is." His face grew red, and he smiled. "Sorry, that sounded stupid. Anyway. You were really great."

"Thank you," I said again. I couldn't think of anything more to say.

"Mitch, there you are," Margaret said as she hurried to his side. "I lost you somehow." She glanced at me. "Hello, dear. What a beautiful concert. Your piano piece was lovely." Her eyebrows furrowed. "Have we met before?" she asked, then recognition bloomed on her face. "Oh yes—you stopped by the house a while back to talk to Mitch."

Mitch looked at me in surprise.

"Really? Was that you? Anne Kelly? I tried to call you back a couple of times, but the number wasn't working. What did you need?"

"I . . . um . . . ," I stumbled over the words, trying to find a viable excuse. "It's Annie, actually. Annie May. I'm sorry for the confusion of my note, but I was just trying to, um, talk to you about your service trip. I heard about it from Bishop Michaels, and it sounded really amazing."

He smiled.

"Oh, were you there last Sunday?"

"No, I missed it. I heard it was great, though. Really inspiring."

"It was a lot of fun. I met some really cool people in your ward. One of them invited us to come to the concert. He was—oh, you know him. The cellist. Sam."

"I thought it sounded nice, so I talked Mitch into bringing me," Margaret cut in. She was eyeing me with a question in her eyes. I knew I was hanging on every word, no matter how mundane or insignificant, and at the mention of Sam's name I swayed just a bit. The reality of the whole situation was sinking in, and I started to feel a little faint. Mitch must have seen it in my face.

"Are you sure you're okay? You didn't get hurt, did you?"

"Why, what happened?" Margaret asked in concern.

"A couple of kids were goofing around and she got knocked over, practically trampled." I smiled a little at the exaggeration.

"I'm fine. Just tired, I guess. It's been a long day."

"Well, I can imagine. A big show like this must take a lot of preparation, and you are all very talented," Margaret said. "Are you planning on studying music in college?" I knew she was just making small talk, but it seemed very important suddenly that I clarify.

"Maybe, but whatever I study, I'm staying here to do it. I'm not going away to school or anything."

"Um, okay. That sounds great," Mitch said, obviously confused about my sudden vehemence.

"Well, if you're sure you're okay, then it's time for me to go. For us to go," he corrected. The words hit me with heartbreaking clarity.

I stood in the middle of the high school foyer, surrounded by people, some friends, some strangers, a few family members somewhere, and I looked into the eyes of my husband and best friend, the father of my children. He was my past and my future. *I will be with you. We will be together. I promise you.* Maybe he would see something of what I was thinking. Maybe not. But I vowed that my promise would come true.

I cleared my throat and spoke out loud. "Thank you. I'll see you around." They were tiny words, but they were a start. The rest would follow down the road. I knew that Margaret was saying good-bye, but I couldn't look away.

"Good-bye," Mitch said, smiling.

Here it was. "Good-bye." Then I watched him walk out the door, his mother's arm tucked into his, caring for her as he cared for everyone, including me, throughout his life.

"Who was that?" Corrie asked.

I hadn't noticed her approach. "That's the man I'm going to marry," I told her.

She rolled her eyes. "Ha, ha, funny. Come on. I told your mom I would find you." She grabbed my hand and pulled me back toward the auditorium. She was bubbling over with chatter about the performance and who had said what about whom.

"Then Sam left with Miranda. She's such a witch. Did you know that she actually had her mother lower the neckline of her choir dress? It's repulsive."

"He left with her?" I asked.

"Yeah, sorry. I thought you two were working things out. It seems like you've been joined at the hip lately. So what's up with that?"

"Uh, we decided it wasn't going to work out," I said, numbly. I swayed then, again, barely catching my balance.

"Are you okay? Annie, you are white as a ghost," she said.

"I'm just a little lightheaded. I think I need to sit down," I murmured. I sank into the nearest seat at the back of the auditorium, and Corrie hurried forward to where my mom and sisters were waiting for me. She spoke to Mom, and they walked quickly back.

"What's going on, honey?" Mom asked.

"I'm dizzy."

"It's probably all the excitement and the crowds. Let's just get you home and to bed. You'll be fine in the morning."

I nodded.

"See you tomorrow, Corrie," I said over my shoulder as we left.

"Bye," she called, then hurried off to find her dad.

Chapter

36

I floated home, unaware of the jabbering of my siblings or the congratulations of my mother. The dizziness continued, but mostly I was just filled with a deep sense of gratitude for the gift I had been given. I responded when I was spoken to, but I had no idea what I answered. I was vaguely aware that we had arrived at home, and Mom walked me up to my room.

"Good night, honey. Get some sleep, okay?" she said as she walked away. She stopped, turned, and came back, wrapping me in a tight bear hug. My mom wasn't usually so physically affectionate with me, not since things had become more strained between us, but the past few weeks had brought those old walls down, and the sweetness of the moment was icing on the cake for the evening.

"I love you, Mom," I said against her shoulder.

"I love you, too, honey," she said. She patted my back and released me. "Bed right away, okay?" she reminded.

"Definitely," I went into my room and closed the door.

I stripped my clothes off quickly and yanked on my sweats. I sank down onto the bed, pulling the bobby pins out of my hair at the same time. I was physically, mentally, and emotionally exhausted, but I was enveloped in the glow of my moment with Mitch.

There was sorrow, too, as I thought about Sam, but I knew that what he had done had been freely given. It wasn't enough to remove the pain, but at least I was at peace.

I sank down on the floor by my bed, clasped my hands together, letting the tears come, and poured out my heart to God. "Dear Heavenly Father, thank you. Thank you for letting me see Mitch again.

Thank you for my family. I miss them so much, Father, but I know you'll bring me safely back to them." I went on, pouring out my gratitude for the moments I'd had with Mitch tonight. I thanked the Lord for my parents and Hannah, Rachel, and even Dan. I thanked him for Corrie. Then I thanked him for Sam. I prayed that Sam would be happy and successful and that he would find love. Finally, exhausted, I crawled into bed and pulled the blankets up, sinking gratefully into the pillow.

I was just starting to drift into sleep when I heard the door open, and my dad came slowly in.

"Dad, what are you doing up?" I asked, sitting up in concern. "I thought you were sleeping."

"Stay there. I'm fine. I just wanted to talk to you first." He made his way slowly toward me, taking each step carefully, but I could see that he had regained some of his strength. He sat down on the side of the bed with a grunt. "It's stupid how much that little walk tires me," he grumbled, then waved away my concerned comment before I could get it out.

"I hear it was a great night. Your mom said you looked like an angel and sounded even better. I'm real proud of you, baby cakes."

"Thanks, Dad. It was a great night." I hugged my knees and thought again of Mitch's hand raising me to my feet, of his eyes on mine, the feel of his fingers in my hand.

"Well, your mom said you were exhausted, but it looks to me like you got some of your spark back. That's good. I've been missing that lately."

"Yeah, me, too."

"Well, I won't keep you up. I just wanted to say good night and tell you that I'll be there, front row, for the next big show. Deal?"

"Deal. Thanks, Dad," I said with a smile. He grinned and patted my arm, then stood up and made his way slowly to the door.

"'Night, Annie," he said.

"Good night."

The door clicked shut behind him, and I lay back down, a feeling of warmth and satisfaction sweeping over me. My brief conversation with Mitch chased itself around my head as I fell asleep, and my dreams were full of him. At one point in the night I woke up enough to realize that I could still call Sam first thing in the morning and really thank him, and say good-bye.

A random thought popped into my head, waking me for a moment. "Good-bye" had been the key all along. The thought faded and was replaced by more dreams of Mitch and the girls and me on our vacation to the beach. I could hear the rush of the waves and the girls as they giggled and chased each other, and Mitch as he tried to find seashells, and the sound of the birds all around me.

The birdsong grew louder, and I woke with a start to sunlight streaming in through the window. The birds were singing in the maple tree outside, even though the branches were bare and the air was turning frosty. I rolled over to look at the clock and nearly fell on the floor. My back screamed out in protest as the ache of sleeping on the horrible green sofa all night made itself known.

I jumped up, instantly regretting it as the muscles in my back cramped at the movement, and stared at the couch in shock, then down at my hands. The baby-soft skin was gone, replaced by just a hint of wrinkles, and a lot more freckles. My nails were longer and my hands much thinner. I patted my belly, my hips, my waist—they were all smaller.

I was thinner and definitely older. I was home.

Chapter
37

I am home. The words tumbled around in my head, and I rushed to the corner table where my purse was sitting and dug through it frantically, looking for my wallet.

I pulled it out and, flipping it open, sank down on the couch with a sob. There in the place of honor was the picture I always carried with me, only this time it was different. Just like the original, this picture showed Mitch and me and our girls, but, unlike the original, there was no tiny picture of James cut out and placed in the corner of the photo sleeve. No, he was there, cradled in Mitch's arms, his tiny hand wrapped around his daddy's finger.

James had never met his daddy. As I examined that picture and searched for answers, a miraculous stream of memories came pouring in, surrounding me with their familiarity. They were like two rivers, both leading from the same lake and arriving at the same ocean but taking different paths. I could remember both sets of memories—they were mine after all—and they were mostly the same, with only a few differences.

The memories of meeting and marrying Mitch were the same. Our honeymoon, our first apartment—these were all the same, but there was much more music in them. I taught voice lessons and eventually started a children's choir that I still ran. I could name the place where we held our rehearsals and the names and faces of the children. It was my business, and I loved it.

I rocked back, clutching the photos as more memories came to the surface. The births of my three children were there, except that in the new memories Mitch was at James's birth. How was that possible? A tiny flicker of an insane hope bloomed in me. Maybe . . .

But no. The hope was dashed as I remembered Mitch's death. His funeral. Only this time I stood by his graveside with Margaret, still alive, and all three children as we said good-bye to our husband and father and son. The tears fell as the memory washed over me. I had replayed this scene millions of times in my head, the original version. It was nothing new, but it still hurt.

And yet the hurt was less bitter. It was tempered by the memory of all of the times that Mitch had played with James, by all those extra memories of our family together, and finally by the treasured memory of him lying in his hospital bed and opening his eyes one last time, his mouth forming the words, *Love you.* I saw myself kissing his hand, his cheek, his head, his lips, and whispering, "Good-bye."

I let the tears pour down my cheeks, silent, healing tears that washed away the anger and the desperation. When they slowed I felt as if they had filled me somehow, giving me energy instead of sucking it away. I stared at the picture again, and I noticed that there were more behind it.

I flipped through them quickly, soaking up the wonderful beauty of the smiling faces of my children, the laughing eyes of Mitch, and one picture with Margaret reading to all three of my children. *That* was a miracle.

Then I heard a voice down the hall.

"Grandma, are you making pancakes?"

The wallet flew from my fingers, and I jumped off the couch.

"Mallory?" I called. I ran to the door, throwing it open with a bang. Mallory was standing in the hall in her nightgown, bare feet poking out from beneath the ruffle. Her hair was tumbling down her back in messy waves.

"Morning, Mom. Are you hungry? I think Grandma is making pancakes." Her words were cut off as she yawned.

"Baby!" I cried out and ran to her. I dropped to my knees and wrapped my arms around her, burying my face against her chest. "Oh, honey, I missed you so much. How are you? Have you been having a good time? Where are your brother and sister?" I couldn't hold her close enough. She smelled so good.

"Sheesh, Mom. Don't call me 'baby.' I'm almost a teenager." Her voice was exasperated, but she hugged me back. "Jenna and James are still sleeping."

She pointed over her shoulder at the room that had been Rachel's and now served as a guest room for the grandkids. I grabbed her hand and pulled her along with me as I rushed into the room. James peeked out of his crib, bleary-eyed and drowsy, and Jenna's hair was just visible above the blankets on the bed.

"Oh, my children!" I cried out, and I rushed to pull James from his bed. He snuggled into my shoulder and wrapped his warm baby arms around my neck. Mallory tried to leave, but I grabbed her and pulled her along with me, and we crashed onto the bed, waking poor Jenna from a deep sleep. I gathered them to me and kissed and hugged every part of them that I could reach. Kissing turned to tickling, and we laughed as tears poured down my face. I couldn't tell which were tears of mirth and which of sorrow or joy or relief. It was all mixed together in one amazing explosion of living.

"Mom, I'm hungry," Jenna said as our giggles slowed somewhat.

"Me, too, baby cakes. Let's go eat some breakfast."

Epilogue

How do I look?" I asked. Mom, Mallory, and Jenna were all sitting on my bed. Mom was wearing jeans, her hair pulled up into a ponytail, and she was lounging with James, a picture book open on her lap.

"Amazing," Mallory said, admiring the new red dress and spiky black heels that Corrie had pushed me into buying.

Jenna clapped. "Pretty."

Mom just gave me a big smile and two thumbs up, but her eyes spoke volumes.

"Are you sure? This isn't too over the top?" I fidgeted with the hem of the dress.

"No, it's perfect. You're going to knock him over," said Mallory.

"Maybe I should wear a sweater." I walked back to my closet and started searching for anything that could work with the rest of the outfit.

I heard Mom give James to Mallory and follow me. She put her hands on my shoulders and turned me around.

"Honey. You look fabulous. You don't need a sweater. Just go and have fun. It's just another experience, right? What is it that your father always says?"

"I know. First day of the rest of my life. I get it. If you're sure . . ."

"I'm sure. We'll be fine here. Hannah is going to stop by later and bring Travis Junior over to play with his cousins, and with Dad and the rest of the boys watching football tonight I'm in no rush to get home.

So stay late, have fun. Just relax, okay?" She kissed me on the cheek and shoved me gently toward the door.

"Okay, I'm going, but call me if you need anything."

"Go!" Mom called with a laugh.

I walked downstairs to the front door but froze, unable to make myself reach for the doorknob. What was I thinking? I had loved two men in my life, both of them perfect for me in their own individual ways. It was ludicrous to think that I could be so lucky as to find a third. Mitch was gone. Sam had disappeared off the face of the earth, it seemed. That part of my life was over, and I was actually okay with it. So why was I inflicting this upon myself?

I knew the answer. It was the same reason I had started doing so many other things out of my comfort zone—taking dance classes and going to movies and now dating. It was all because I wanted to show my children that life continues on and that they could do anything they put their minds to. Dad had his own mantra, his phrase that gave him strength, and now I had mine as well.

"I can do hard things," I told myself again, and I forced myself to reach for the doorknob and stepped outside.

It was a short walk to Shelley's where we were all going to meet before dinner and dancing, just four houses down the street, and it sped by far too quickly. Next thing I knew, I was knocking on her door. My hand trembled slightly, and I repeated my mantra to steady myself. Shelley opened the door.

"Wow, Anne. You look amazing, darlin'. Great dress. Doesn't she look great, Pete?" she called to her husband. He looked up from his paper and grunted, his usual verbose response. Shelley glared at him and turned an overly bright smile back to me. "See, he thinks you look amazing, too. Come on in. He's not here yet, but he called and said he's just a couple of minutes away. Sit down and make yourself at home. Do you want something to drink?"

"No, thanks," I said, but I followed her into the kitchen. I paced back and forth while she poured herself a diet soda.

"Anne, will you calm down already? It's just a date," Shelley laughed.

"I know. I know," I said, but I kept pacing. "Tell me about him again."

"What else do you want to know? He's divorced, with one child. He's a musician . . ."

I stopped pacing. "You never told me he was a musician." At least we would have something to talk about.

"Yeah, plays the cello or something and just moved back to town." At the word "cello," my heart flipped over.

"Um, where does Pete know him from?" I asked quietly. I couldn't quite picture Pete being friends with a cellist.

"Oh, it's the funniest story. I guess they met through work, and when he found out where we lived, he started asking all kinds of questions. Turns out he was planning on moving here, like I said, and he and Pete just hit it off. He even offered us symphony tickets," Shelley said with a laugh. "I couldn't convince Pete to take me, though." She sipped at her drink.

An impossible hope was forming in my heart. "Shelley," I said casually, fighting to make my voice more than a whisper. "I just realized that you never told me his name."

She lowered her glass. "Really? Funny. It's Sam Campbell."

There was a knock at the door. "Oh, that'll be him," she said. She walked around me to the door, unaware that I was frozen in place, my heart somewhere near my shoes.

Campbell. It was his mother's maiden name. In all my searching I had looked for Sam Harris or even Sam Sharp. It never occurred to me that he might change his name, but with Leonard in the mix it made perfect sense. Was it really him?

Shelley opened the door, and I forced myself to turn and look up.

"There you are," she said. "We were beginning to think you weren't coming. Weren't we, Anne?" She took a step back, and he came into view.

His shoulders and chest were broader, and he had grown at least two more inches. There were a few laugh lines around his eyes, and his hair had receded ever so slightly, giving him a higher forehead, but those were the same lips, the same eyes.

Those eyes weren't surprised to see me. It was as if he had been expecting it. I began to suspect why he and Pete had bonded so instantly, but I didn't really care how this had happened. I was too busy drinking in the sight of him. I let it fill all the parched, lonely places in my heart.

"Sam?" I managed to whisper. He smiled at me with all of the love that I had seen so long ago. It had been six months for me and twenty years for him, but it was like we had never parted.

I found all the strength I needed then to walk to him and throw my arms around him. I kissed him long and hard, reveling in his arms around me and the feel of his lips on mine. I was vaguely aware of Pete laughing in his chair—and Shelley's shocked comments next to us— but I didn't care that we had an audience.

This was my Sam, and he still loved me. I had seen it in his eyes, and I could feel it in the kiss that he was so willing to return. This time nothing would stand in our way. He was mine, and I would never, ever let him go again.

About the Author

EMILY GRAY CLAWSON describes herself as an author, mother, and youth mentor. Born and raised in Utah, she is passionate about her faith and great books and will share her love of both with anyone who will listen. Emily began writing at the age of seven, creating homemade picture books that she peddled from door to door. She self-published her first novel, *Things Hoped For,* and is collaborating with Jennifer Graves on a book entitled *A Sister's Witness: The Powell Family Tragedy.* With her husband, Richard, Emily founded two youth leadership programs, Handmaidens of Virtue and Mastering Knighthood. Trained in vocal performance in college, she has enjoyed including aspects of her training in this book. Emily and Richard are the parents of four children and live in Taylorsville, Utah.

Learn more about Emily at www.emilygrayclawson.com.